NOVEL 11, BOOK 18

ALSO BY DAG SOLSTAD

•

Armand V.

Professor Andersen's Night

T. Singer

DAG SOLSTAD

Novel 11, Book 18

translated from the Norwegian by Sverre Lyngstad

A NEW DIRECTIONS BOOK

First published in English by Harvill Secker, an imprint of Vintage. Vintage is part of the Penguin Random House Group of companies.

Manufactured in the United States of America
First published by New Directions in 2021 as NDP1504

Library of Congress Cataloging-in-Publication Data
Names: Solstad, Dag, 1941– author. | Lyngstad, Sverre, translator.
Title: Novel 11, book 18 / Dag Solstad ; translated from the Norwegian by Sverre Lyngstad.
Other titles: Ellevte roman, bok atten. English | Novel eleven, book eighteen
Description: New York : A New Directions Book, 2021.
Identifiers: LCCN 2021001797 | ISBN 9780811228268 (paperback) | ISBN 9780811228299 (ebook)
Classification: LCC PT8951.29.05 E4413 2021 | DDC 839.823/74—dc23
LC record available at https://lccn.loc.gov/2021001797

10 9 8 7 6 5 4 3 2 1

New Directions Books are published for James Laughlin
by New Directions Publishing Corporation
80 Eighth Avenue, New York 10011

NOVEL 11, BOOK 18

When this story begins, Bjørn Hansen has just turned fifty and is waiting for someone at the Kongsberg Railway Station. It has now been four years since he separated from Turid Lammers, with whom he had lived for fourteen years, from the very moment when he arrived at Kongsberg, which before that time barely existed on the map for him. He now lives in a modern flat in the center of Kongsberg, a mere stone's throw from the railway station. When he arrived at Kongsberg eighteen years ago, he had only a few personal belongings, such as clothes and shoes, plus crates and crates of books. When he moved out of the Lammers villa, he also took away with him only personal possessions, such as clothes and shoes, besides crates and crates of books That was his luggage. Dostoyevsky. Pushkin. Thomas Mann. Céline. Borges. Tom Kristensen. Márquez. Proust. Singer. Heinrich Heine. Malraux, Kafka, Kundera, Freud, Kierkegaard, Sartre, Camus, Butor.

When he had thought about Turid Lammers in the four years which had passed since the breakup, it had been with a sense of relief that it was over. At the same time he'd had to admit, with an amazement that verged on grief, that he was no longer capable either of understanding or bringing back why he had been taken with her. It is beyond doubt, however, that he had been. Otherwise, why would he have broken his marriage to Tina Korpi and abandoned her and their two-year-old son to follow Turid Lammers to Kongsberg, in the secret hope that she would have him? It was because of Turid Lammers that he had ended up at Kongsberg. Without her, or his now forgotten enthrallment by her, he would never have ended up here. Never. His life would have been altogether different. It would never have occurred to him to apply for the position of town treasurer at Kongsberg—in fact, he would not have dreamed of applying for a position as treasurer at all, but would probably have continued in the ministry, made a passable career there, and today in all likelihood would have been head of a government office or have moved on to a high position in the Communications Administration, the Norwegian State Railways or something of the sort. But never town treasurer. Never Kongsberg.

It troubled him that he was unable to bring back the fascination which Turid Lammers had had for him when he first met her. A skinny, nervous woman—that was how he remembered her. When they met she had just returned from France, where she had lived for seven years, with a wrecked marriage behind her. She settled in Oslo and immediately took a lover. The lover was him. Was it his fascination with the effect that women's nerves have on their surroundings that had ensnared him? Those restless mood swings? After half a year her father died, and she moved back to the provincial town she had come from, Kongsberg. Here she settled down in an old villa, took over the management of a florist's with her elder sister, and took a job as teacher at Kongsberg Secondary School, where she taught French, English and drama.

Her father died in September. She went home for the funeral and the settlement of the estate, and returned to Oslo after one week. For a month she lived as before. But then she suddenly decided to move back to Kongsberg. She told her lover on Wednesday evening and by Sunday she was gone. When she said she intended to move, he first felt relief. At long last he could restore normal order to his life. He was married to Tina Korpi and they had a two-year-old son. He had not told Tina about Turid, it was a secret erotic adventure on his part. Actually it suited him well that she went away now, to Kongsberg and out of his life, leaving nothing more behind in his consciousness than the memory of a moment of stolen happiness.

But then he got to thinking that he couldn't let her down. He had to go to Kongsberg, to her, otherwise he would come to regret it for the rest of his life. Indeed, the absolute certainty that he would have regrets made returning to Tina and their son, to continue as before but now without a secret love, impossible. And so he disclosed his secret to his wife and cut loose from his marriage. Aside from the relief he had initially felt when Turid said she was now going home for good, there was also his sense that it could not last; he had already then seen clearly what fourteen years later would result in his leaving her. He had no illusions that she would give him happiness. But when it dawned on him that she really was gone, he missed her so terribly that he was seized by a veritably moral urge to remain close to this woman who was constantly sending out nervous signals to her surroundings, who was never at rest, who was full of ideas, all the time, every hour of the day.

It is possible that he told Tina he had found love and that he could not betray it. In all likelihood he did. It bothered him that he could recall nothing about Turid Lammers from that time to justify these big words. Apart from a few insignificant episodes, such as he and Turid walking arm in arm along the pavement somewhere. Then Turid catches sight of a banana peel, right in front of her on the pavement. She bends down without letting go of his arm and picks it up. Then she flings it into the middle of the street and says, merrily: "I hope the cars will skid on it!" Good God, he had thought (then or later), this is her way of solving her problems! He was employed in a ministry, as he had been ever since he took his university degree in economics six years previously, and had already been promoted to office manager, no more than thirty-two years old. His lover was also thirty-two, a teacher. And so she picked up the banana peel from the pavement and simply flung it somewhere else. At the cars. Completely wacky. He must have been fascinated. But also uneasy, at any rate with a view to possibly sharing his life with her (but that had to be later). Was it episodes like this that made him tell Tina that he had found love and could not betray it? The alternative would have been to say that he was having an adventure and couldn't give it up. That, however, he could not have said, despite the fact that it expressed to perfection why Bjørn Hansen—a poor boy from a Norwegian coastal town, this successful young civil servant in one of our ministries—left his wife and two-year-old son to set out for Kongsberg and an uncertain future. It was his obsession with the adventure that had sucked him in, so intensely that he could barely breathe, and not his love for Turid Lammers. The allure of it. Deep down Bjørn Hansen knew that the most desirable happiness on this earth was a brief happiness, and now he was experiencing it by seeking out Turid Lammers secretly in her little flat at St. Hanshaugen in Oslo. He had never lived so intensely before, because he knew he was in a place where he would not stay for long. It was a dangerous game. Stolen happiness. And since Turid Lammers was the object of all this stolen happiness, he also started saying to himself that it was his love for her that he could not betray. But it wasn't true. Turid Lammers was nothing apart from the adventure, the circumstances surrounding their relationship. Her mimicry, her glances, her gestures, which would send shudders through him, those small wrists, so beautiful and French in their grace, her way of walking—everything received its luster from the circumstances surrounding their relationship. He knew all that. To tell the truth, he was fully aware of it. He had played this game quite consciously, cultivating these stolen moments. He ought to have told his wife: I cannot possibly be certain that this is love, because I barely know her. I know her only from specific situations, where she is the object of my fascination. But these situations fulfill so many of my innermost desires, well, so much of what I expect from life, that now, when she has betrayed these situations by breaking out of them, I have to set out after her in an attempt to find her again.

The only thing he regretted about this break was that he had not told his wife exactly how things were. Otherwise he accepted that everything had turned out as it did. He still recognized, eighteen years afterward, that he had done the right thing in abandoning an unsuspecting wife and his small child sleeping in an adjacent room. In order to look for the woman who represented adventure to him, even though he knew that the adventure was now over by the very fact that he was cutting loose from his marriage to follow Turid Lammers. He had no hopes of recovering what had been, but he wanted to preserve the memory of it, of her, that is, to breathe in the same room as her. He could not let her down. He had discovered in this deliberate infidelity an intensity and a suspense that he could usually only observe with fascination, but without fully understanding, in art and literature.

So he had left. After telling Tina Korpi that he was a prisoner of love and had to follow its commands. Tina Korpi seemed to be in a state of shock. Stunned, so to speak, she sat on a chair just staring at him as she repeated, time and again, "So that was why, I should've known." He had feared that there would be harrowing scenes, and especially that, while it was taking place, they would scream loudly at one another and wake up their son, who was lying in the adjacent room, so that they would have to go in and soothe him and that he, perhaps, would have to pick him up. But that did not happen. Bjørn Hansen packed a few personal belongings, which he took to the car, walking back and forth several times, while she, stunned, was still sitting on her chair every time he came back, repeating, like a wail, "So that was why." Ready at last, he had gone.

He drove to Drammen, under the amber light from the street lamps suspended over the E18, through the town along the eastern bank of the Drammen River, and then up toward Hokksund, still driving along the eastern bank of the Drammen River. At Hokksund there was a fork in the road, with one road leading across the river toward Kongsberg, Notodden, Numedal and Upper Telemark—the one he would take. But before doing so he stopped outside Eikerstua, a roadside pub just before the fork, and went in. Though it was late in the evening, there were still plenty of customers, eating open meat patty sandwiches and drinking coffee, car owners like himself or lorry drivers, their heavy, massive vehicles parked in front of the pub. Bjørn Hansen went straight over to the telephone booth and called Turid Lammers. He felt very nervous as he pushed coins into the slot and dialled the number, for he had not told her in advance that he was on his way. ("I do not want to be the lover of a married man," Turid Lammers had said when she moved to Kongsberg, in a perfectly sober tone which had given him no reason whatsoever to think that she wished he would contribute his share to her not having to.) He heard her voice, while at the same time hearing the kroner pieces rattle into the box, so that he could talk and know that she heard him. He told her what had happened and that he was in a roadside pub some twelve miles north of Drammen, near the exit to Kongsberg. He asked if he could come and she said yes.

He took his seat in the car again and drove toward Kongsberg. All at once he was in the middle of Norway, the inhospitable, wooded, remote and (except for those who live there) out-of-the-way Norway, even though he was only forty-five miles from the nation's capital. It was in the middle of winter, with a heavy snowfall. The road was narrow, though it was a state highway, slippery and winding. High snowbanks left by the plow; cold, compact snow. Flat fields buried in white darkness, gorges and hollows. Scattered farms. Spruce forests. A lone lamp in the night, fixed on the wall of a haphazardly placed modern one-story building, swept by white whirling snow. Frozen lakes. Icebound rivers. Bedraggled spruces. Icicles hanging from crags that dropped steeply over the roadway and were illuminated by the headlights of Bjørn Hansen's car. The trip required far more time than he had calculated, because he had to maintain a low speed in this wintry landscape, which he bored into deeper and deeper along the narrow, winding and slippery road, until suddenly, on a steep downhill slope, he found himself on the outskirts of a town. Soon thereafter he turned off the main road and drove into the illuminated streets of Kongsberg.

It was late in the evening, but there was a surprising number of people to be seen, due to the fact that the last movie screening had just ended; it was ten past eleven. He drove around rather randomly in search of a taxi stand. He found one near the railway station and parked there. He walked over to a taxi driver who sat in his cab waiting his turn. He read out Turid Lammers's address from a slip of paper and the cabby gave him a meticulous explanation as to how to get there. Five minutes later Bjørn Hansen had parked in front of a large but rather run-down villa which, judging by the address, was where Turid Lammers lived.

She did not stand in the doorway waiting for him. He rang the bell, and some time passed, he thought, before she answered. But when she did, she seemed glad to see him. She had made a fire on the hearth. She was waiting for him with food and drink. She seemed calm and relaxed, far more relaxed than he had expected to find her in the vast drafty villa she had inherited.

As it happened, he would live in this old villa for fourteen years. As Turid Lammers's partner. And he still lived in Kongsberg. Early on he commuted to Oslo, to his job at the ministry. Who was Turid Lammers? In Oslo she had been an attractive woman in the whirl of the big city whom he had met by chance and who fascinated him. Now she had gone back to her roots, had even moved into her childhood home, and lived in surroundings that had only been occasional (and very charming) attributes of her personality earlier on. As her lover in Oslo, he had mostly been interested in the French element of her past, those seven years in France that had made her wiser (he assumed) and simultaneously conferred upon her movements that acquired grace, which he (on account of the adventure that lent them glamour) could not live without. Especially her gestures. That Mediterranean way of using the hands as an aesthetic adjunct to the voice had fascinated him, in an all but childish way, so much so that he had barely listened to what she said, so preoccupied was he by the way she said it. And so he had only en passant got to know the small-town side of her, which then emerged only within the context of her exotic southern manner. A Frenchwoman who talked about her impossible sister at Kongsberg. But now all this became a daily reality for Turid Lammers, and thereby also for Bjørn Hansen. The Lammers family had in its time owned half of Kongsberg and its environs. Forests, farmland, stores, building lots, woodworking factories, etc. But when her father died only a florist's and a service station were left, in addition to the old Lammers villa. The sister got the lucrative service station, managed by her husband, and Turid got, after many ifs and buts, the villa, while the florist's was jointly owned by both sisters. All this led to a wrangling that was not yet over when Bjørn Hansen, after fourteen years, finally moved out of the Lammers villa and acquired his own place. It was basically a question of which sister best represented their legacy, the Lammers name.

On the face of it Turid Lammers was above such matters, and her partner, Bjørn Hansen, thought so too for a long time.

She was antibourgeois in her very being. She despised fussing over money and her sister's way of raking it in, as she put it, meaning it quite sincerely, and when a two-hundred-year-old sauceboat slipped from her hands and broke on the floor at one of the parties they gave in the Lammers villa, causing the sauce to ooze out among the broken porcelain fragments, she laughed, and her eyes sparkled as she exclaimed, "This is a historic moment! Two hundred years fell out of my hands and was reduced to nothing!" To a standing ovation from the guests. But Bjørn Hansen knew that the sight of the broken sauceboat affected her painfully. For when this happened he had lived with her, as her husband, for two years.

That he had not done, however, when he returned from the ministry in Oslo one evening and, slumped over the latest issue of the daily paper, *Lågendalsposten*, during their late dinner, she called attention to an ad. Bjørn Hansen considered himself a slow, introverted and not very spontaneous person. The ad announced an opening: the position as town treasurer at Kongsberg had now become vacant for qualified applicants. Bjørn Hansen read the ad, then gave Turid an inquiring glance. Was there something in the wording of the ad that had awakened her antibureaucratic sense of humor? But Turid again pointed at the ad and said, "For you, my dear. Town treasurer—that would be something for you, wouldn't it?" Bjørn Hansen looked at her again. He laughed. "Well, why not?"

Yes, why not? Why shouldn't he apply for the position of treasurer at Kongsberg, now that he lived there? No sooner said than done. Bjørn Hansen solemnly applied for the position.

What is a town treasurer? A tax collector. He is the one who is responsible for the payment, on time, of the rightful taxes and fees to the State and the local authority, and for taking the necessary measures when that doesn't happen. Originally, being a tax collector was a very high office; it was the bailiff who had that task, and he was the king's man. Later it was the treasurer. He was a municipal public servant, trusted and respected, but he held a position with its roots in the urban community, and the fact that the tax collector was changed from being bailiff to treasurer can be seen as an expression of the State changing its character from a bureaucratic system of government to one based on extensive local democracy. The small-town treasurer in the twentieth century was no high official; he was recruited in the course of the daily routine in the Norwegian town where he worked, usually had no academic education, being a graduate of a business school or commercial college, and had risen through the ranks in the office of the treasurer.

Bjørn Hansen's application was not welcomed by the treasury office employees. With his university degree and experience at the ministry, he was actually overqualified and therefore pulled ahead of two longtime members of the staff who had lately been scowling at each other because both considered themselves qualified to reach the top. Bjørn Hansen snatched the title from under their very noses. And they immediately joined forces against him, from the first day that he—an outsider who lived with Turid Lammers in the Lammers villa, a snob of thirty-two with too many degrees, a softy—had a good look at the office and his colleagues.

He had moved to Kongsberg. And, on a whim, he had applied for the position of town treasurer and got it. In reality, he merely shrugged. Why in the world should he be town treasurer? A treasurer, of all things? Some whim that was, he thought, astounded. But Turid walked through the rooms of the Lammers villa singing, "My husband is town treasurer! My husband is town treasurer! I'm living with the treasurer! I'm living with the treasurer!" Bjørn Hansen gazed at her in admiration. He couldn't help laughing.

There was an audacious element in Turid Lammers's gaiety that fascinated him. Thus encouraged, he went to his daily task, albeit with a shrug. Was he thinking that this job might be a professional dead end, to put it mildly? Well, he knew that, but simply gave a shrug. It was more important for him to find a job at Kongsberg, because he was beginning to get tired of commuting (it was also a strain on their relationship). He wouldn't have minded continuing in the ministry, but not if he lived at Kongsberg. And now he was living at Kongsberg, that was a fact. Bjørn Hansen had grown up in a town by the Oslo Fjord, the son of parents of limited means. He was a poor boy. Nevertheless it seemed natural to him to go to college, on account of his ready wits. He received his maturity certificate at the age of nineteen and, after sixteen months of military service, he had to make up his mind what he wanted to do with his life. Bjørn Hansen decided to go to Oslo to study. In reality, he was mostly interested in art and literature, philosophy and the meaning of life, but he chose to study economics. Chiefly because he had always been good at arithmetic and mathematics, but also because he had a vague feeling that he had to rise and get on in life, so as not to end up in the same poverty as his parents; at any rate, he wanted to get away from their bitter toil, and while he did not equate art and literature, philosophy and the meaning of life with bitter toil, they had, quite simply, an aura of luxury about them. Art and literature were not proper subjects to him, they were interests one could cultivate in one's spare time, not means whereby to acquire a position, which he, with a genuinely unassuming matter-of-factness, saw as the end of academic study. Hence economics. But there were two ways of studying economics—you could become a Bachelor of Commerce (in Bergen) or a political economist (in Oslo). For Bjørn Hansen it had to be political economy. The study of business administration led to employment by private corporations, to the no doubt exciting jungle there, but this was so remote from Bjørn Hansen's own point of departure, his moral and social intelligence, etc., that he did not even consider it. Due to some form of social consciousness, he chose political economy and, consequently, a career in public administration. So he decided to become a servant of the State, for lack of other alternatives.

When he met Turid Lammers, he had been employed in the ministry for six years (Bjørn Hansen always said, "I was employed in the ministry," but never said which one in all the eighteen years that had now gone by since he arrived at Kongsberg), and if someone asked him in which ministry, he replied, "Er, some ministry, I no longer remember exactly which," and couldn't be made to say anything more, even though everyone knew that he was lying and had been about to be promoted. He wouldn't have minded that, viewing it as quite natural, and could easily imagine being assistant or deputy secretary. He felt quite happy in the ministry; he found it exciting to work out budget estimates, and he was not insensitive to the fact that the estimates they were working out, in different variants, would have a practical bearing on the daily lives of hundreds of thousands of Norwegians, a thought which in no way was conducive to losing interest in one's work. It was a sensible kind of work Bjørn Hansen was performing, and he could easily imagine continuing with it. But when Turid encouraged him, merrily, to apply for the position of town treasurer in Kongsberg, he had no problem with bidding farewell to his career in the ministry and he had never missed it during the eighteen years that had passed.

Did he become treasurer for Turid's sake? He would not have done it without her encouragement, at any rate. Without her merriment at the thought that her partner would be the town's treasurer. It was quite mad, Turid's eyes sparkled, and he thought, "I'll do it! Hell, yes, I'll do it!" and instantly felt a wild satisfaction at the thought that he would actually do it. It was the final break with everything that had gone before. It bound him at last to Turid Lammers. To this town. To their relationship here in this large, dilapidated Lammers villa. To the adventure, which had already acquired so many absurd features, and which he was as fascinated by as ever.

But to Turid's (and, for that matter, his own) amazement, he had from the very first moment set about his work with great seriousness—well, almost fervor. Partly because, from the start, he felt the hostility in the treasurer's office from the two employees who had been passed over. To tell the truth, he felt as if he had behaved rather shabbily toward them. It was really their job, after all, they should have competed for it, and the one who didn't get it would forever have borne a grudge against the other and plotted against him intensely, on the quiet, using every low trick imaginable, instead of, as now, joining forces as allies, as time went by even as close friends, and directing all of their ill will toward him, the new treasurer. Having all but strolled into this leadership position (he had sixteen subordinates), he found himself with something to sharpen his wits on. Intrigue and knavery. The amount of mischief a roughly fifty-year-old employee in a treasury office can dream up when he feels he has been played for a fool and prevented from attaining his natural peak as town treasurer, is quite indescribable. And when, as in this case, there were two of a kind—birds of a feather, as they say—the atmosphere at the treasury could at times be more than strained. Instead of being laden with dust, which people usually associate with offices where dry, creaky bureaucrats spend their days, the corners were alive with a festering glow. But this atmosphere hardened him, well, matured him, if not as a human being, at least as a treasurer, and that was, after all, what mattered in this instance. Another reason why Bjørn Hansen invested his position as treasurer at Kongsberg with a seriousness just short of fervor from the very first day, was that this was his work. He had applied for a position and got it. It was not his mission in life, but his job. In Bjørn Hansen's view, work was a necessary evil. As mentioned already, he chose his field of study on the basis of which necessary evil he wanted to qualify himself for. When the job was done, one could devote oneself to life's true meaning, which for Bjørn Hansen was clearly a woman. Living with a woman, Turid Lammers. But first one is obliged to participate in the communal public enterprise that is called work, in order for the wheels to keep turning, society to function, in short, so that there will be steak at the butcher's, schools for children and young people, clothes to put on, light switches in the halls, running water in the taps, radios, on which someone has undertaken to speak, others to make, still others to transport to the store, which someone has decided to open, and when the radio breaks down someone has taken on the task to repair it, allowing the wheels to turn; and when the snow falls on Kongsberg, the excavators are wolfing down the compact banks of snow to allow new snow to pile up, forming fresh banks at the edges of the road, in order for the wheels to continue turning. In the middle of all this, Bjørn Hansen had assumed the task of managing the office that collected the resources necessary for operating the municipality and the State. He had become the State's unrelenting tax collector in this provincial town. A stern servant of the State.

Kongsberg is situated in the middle of Norway by the river Lågen, which runs in a lovely arc through the town and separates Old Kongsberg from New Kongsberg. A handsome bridge connected the two towns, which were decorated with realistic sculptures in praise of work, like mining and rafting. The modern center strongly resembled all other Norwegian towns, its main streets lined with shops where you could buy, in abundance, what modern civilization had to offer, from knitting needles to the latest computer models. This was the bustling part of town. The old center housed most of the city administration, surrounded by decayed wooden buildings from the old days—this was in the early 1970s. A magnificent church on a hill. A venerable police station in an old patrician villa. A dismal prison, along with the rest situated around the church square. Also the fire station, not to forget the Town Hall with its varied functions.

The town was built up around the silver mining industry. The kingdom of Denmark-Norway's only silver mines were located here, and so, in the sixteen hundreds, Christian IV laid the foundation of the town. Thousands of workers and German mining experts, along with Danish officials, lived here. It was nicely situated, surrounded by hills that were green from spring to autumn and white in the winter. The river was blue from spring to autumn and white with ice in the winter. Here lay the Kongsberg Arms Factory and the Royal Mint—which was still producing Norwegian coins—together with other enterprises. There were shops, tradesmen, dentists, attorneys, physicians, functionaries, shop girls, office girls, teachers, municipal employees—and workers. And all of them had to pay taxes.

Bjørn Hansen made himself at home in the town in a surprisingly short time. Even as treasurer. Shortly he had acquired a nodding acquaintance with a number of people he met in the street on his way from the Lammers villa to the Town Hall, where the Treasury was located. He passed this way twice a day, first in the morning, to the office, then in the afternoon, from the office. He spent most of his working hours in the office, interrupted by meetings at the alderman's, where he presented economic reports on the tax revenues to date, while showing how they tallied with the prognoses made in the budget. It was a pleasant life—the job entailed responsibility but was not stressful. It was, on the whole, a set of routines, and if you knew them, everything ran more or less by itself. Not once did he take work home with him. He felt he was met with friendliness everywhere. Few appeared to think of him as an awe-inspiring government authority who ruthlessly cracked down on failure to pay tax arrears and on deficient payment of value-added tax. Few appeared to think of the fact that, when he wrote his name, his signature, on an official sheet of paper, it meant that the government was now demanding its due and would brook no argument. Armed with a sheet of paper with *Bjørn Hansen, Treasurer* on it, his subordinates marched off, rang the bells of private homes, entered courteously and, without listening to any protests, took away TV sets, pieces of furniture and paintings as government security against unpaid tax. He even had businesses and industrial concerns declared bankrupt, with all the consequences this had not only for the unfortunate owners, but even more, it turned out, for those who had worked by the sweat of their brows in these businesses and concerns. Yet when he walked through the streets, people greeted him like a friend, and he returned their greetings in a friendly manner. Despite rumors of internal conflicts in the Treasury, where he, an outsider, was opposed by two venerable and loyal Kongsberg drudges, the new treasurer had a nodding acquaintance with a considerable number of people. It was partly due to the fact that in his line of work he came into contact with many of the town's inhabitants, not least businessmen and people who held public office, but the main reason was that most of those he greeted were members of the same society as he himself, namely, the Kongsberg Theater Society.

Yes, he had become a member of the Kongsberg Theater Society, even an enthusiastic member. It was Turid Lammers who had got him involved. She had acted in amateur theater in her early youth and, having now returned to her roots, she wasted no time in joining the Kongsberg Theater Society, of which many of the friends from her youth were still members. During the years she had been away Turid Lammers had done things and improved herself. She had studied theater, both in

Norway and in France, and now taught drama at the Kongsberg Secondary School, in addition to the more common subjects of English and French. She was an asset from day one and had been accepted with open arms; it was not long before she suggested that Bjørn Hansen should join them. He hesitated, telling her that he was not an actor, but she replied that there were so many other things he could do; it was first and foremost a question of being part of a milieu. But Bjørn Hansen thought that if he were not an actor he would be somehow second-rate in that milieu, and he did not want that. Turid protested loudly, saying she was convinced that he could become a good actor, he simply hadn't tried. Besides, they were all equals in the Kongsberg Theater Society, that was a principle; the main roles were given out by turns, so that everyone got involved; and, of course, there were also so many other things that had to be done to put on a whole evening's entertainment. The upshot was that Bjørn joined the Society, accompanied his partner to rehearsals, took out membership, and found himself an insider.

The Kongsberg Theater Society put on one production a year. They played it six times in late autumn at the Kongsberg Cinema, after having been in preparation since Christmas the previous year. Bjørn Hansen's first job was as a sort of odd-job-man-*cum*-stagehand. He ran errands, took care of applications, helped organize the ticket sales, served as cashier, helped to prepare the budget, and talked up the coming performance at the Treasury and the Town Hall, and during the performance he could be found behind the scenes busily moving scenery and changing the sets while the curtain was down, and everyone in the auditorium could hear the shuffling of heavy furniture being dragged across the stage, and a loud thud as an armchair was put down by a perspiring Bjørn Hansen. Who, in the next moment, when the curtain went up again, found himself backstage, anxiously waiting to see how the next scene would go, whether the public would be drawn in, whether the singing dentist, Herman Busk, would transcend himself this evening as he nervously took his last steps toward the footlights, past Bjørn Hansen, who, deeply moved, whispered "Good luck," barely audible to anybody but himself.

Yes, he was drawn into it. He liked the milieu that came with putting on amateur productions. He got to know people. Turid and he had acquired a shared leisure interest, which almost became a passion. Turid became a leading light in the Theater Society—being a drama teacher, she was, after all, almost a professional. She loved to appear on stage and knew how to hold an audience in the hollow of her hand; Bjørn Hansen would stand in the wings and observe how the citizens of Kongsberg allowed themselves to be thoroughly charmed by his partner, the woman for whose sake he found himself here, and he felt very proud. He observed her when she left the stage after having conquered her public, her whole body trembling and her face having a dreamy, inward expression. "Superb," he whispered, causing her to give a start before hurrying on to the dressing room and preparation for her next appearance. Turid Lammers's return to her native town, Kongsberg, had certainly benefited the Kongsberg Theater Society. Indeed, she became its central player. She knew how everything worked, both front- and backstage. But she was no prima donna. In fact, she never took the lead, leaving that to others. She chose to shine in minor roles, albeit central minor roles, but they were not main roles. The others always encouraged her to take the lead, but she refused. It wouldn't be right, she said. But offstage the main role was hers, her ideas concerning costumes always prevailed. Choice of material became, in the final analysis, her choice. If the suggested stage director was not to the liking of Turid Lammers, he simply did not get to be director. The Lammers villa became a natural center for the Society's preparations: here costumes were sewn, ideas conceived, parties hosted. Here the friends of the Kongsberg Theater Society came and went pretty much as they pleased, at any hour of the day or night. Here came Jan Grotmol, an Adonis employed by the railways. Here came Brian Smith, an engineer at the Kongsberg Arms Factory and a guaranteed success with his deep bass voice and his broken Norwegian. And Mrs. Smith, who spoke only English but was educated as a needlework teacher (lace). Here came Dr. Schiøtz from the hospital and Sandsbråten, the old postmaster. Here came the beautiful women to whom Turid Lammers granted the main roles, to their everlasting gratitude. Here came Herman Busk, the dentist, who happened to become Bjørn Hansen's best friend, as well as elderly shop assistants, young students, gardeners, dairymen and, not least, numerous teachers of all ages and both genders, from all of the schools in the Kongsberg district, along with representatives of the health service. And two laborers.

The atmosphere was one of enthusiasm, though it did have a tendency toward arrogance. The friends of the Kongsberg Theater Society looked upon themselves as creative spirits and considered their hobby as a vocation, because in their view everyone possessed an animating power that was frequently suppressed or tamed, but which could unfold freely in the theater, through acting things out, through play. Man as player, or *homo ludens*, as they said, was their ideal, which it became Bjørn Hansen's fate in life to represent as well. For he had already become one of them, not only in his capacity as Turid Lammers's companion, but also because he fully shared their fascination with standing behind the curtain before the performance and peeking into the auditorium through a narrow opening in it in order to see the public flowing to their seats in this illuminated cinema in anticipation of the curtain rising. The Society played either farces or operettas; there was controversy among its members every year whether they should perform straight farces (especially comedies of mistaken identity, where success was assured) or whether they should risk taking on an operetta, which was more ambitious, and usually an operetta or a musical came out the winner. *My Fair Lady. Summer in Tyrol. Oklahoma. Bør Børson.* This was in the 1970s. Bjørn Hansen debuted in *Oklahoma*, as a walk-on. A member of the chorus, he danced around in a cowboy outfit, having learned a few simple steps, and sang with what little voice he had. It worked out nicely. Later he participated every year and could honestly say that few Norwegians had sung the refrain of more operetta tunes in public than he. Although he had never before stood on a stage, it worked out nicely. It was fairly bewildering, but Turid Lammers said she was not surprised, adding that, if they had not been living together as man and wife, she would have nominated him for a really big role next year.

This was how Bjørn Hansen's existence had shaped up. This was his life. At Kongsberg. With Turid Lammers, this woman he had to live with because he feared he would otherwise regret everything. Turid Lammers was the life and soul of the circle. Her beauty and sophistication dazzled everyone. Why didn't they get married? Because Bjørn Hansen assumed that Turid Lammers would consider such a question coming from him to be infra dig. Hadn't he left everything and come to Kongsberg, to her, to live with her without any guarantees? To the others in the circle, Bjørn Hansen's presence in the Lammers villa was completely natural. He was a man who had been offered the chance to leave everything, and to do so in the company of Turid Lammers. When Bjørn Hansen saw Turid Lammers shining so brightly in the surroundings of the Kongsberg Theater Society, he too thought that way. But he had also caught sight of something else about her, namely, that she was all the time under the influence of something that had long ago come to an end, which did not exist. Turid Lammers was not going anywhere, there was no direction to her life, except to remain where she was and sparkle. All this enthusiasm, all these plans, all this energy finding an outlet every hour of the day, in the classroom, in the florist's, in the Society, in her life with Bjørn Hansen—all this had no meaning beyond itself.

Was he playing a dangerous game? In any case, he awoke one night to find her side of the bed empty. It might have been about a year after he arrived in Kongsberg. He had become accustomed to his new life. He saw that she wasn't there. He looked at the time. Four. She had gone out in the evening, to a rehearsal. He couldn't sleep, just lay there twisting and turning. When she came it was half past five. Where had she been? Where she had been? Was she not a free human being? Bjørn Hansen could not bring himself to enter into a discussion of human freedom on such premises and went to sleep. When he got up two hours later, she sat at the breakfast table, as usual. She revealed that she had been talking with Jan at his place, his digs, all night. Bjørn Hansen nodded. Jan was the strikingly beautiful railway employee who played Sigismund in *Summer in Tyrol*, which they were rehearsing; he had a scene with Turid Lammers. "I see."—"I see, I see, is that anything to get jealous about?"—"I'm not jealous!"—"You're not jealous?" Turid Lammers laughed. Aloud, scornfully. She kept at it until Bjørn Hansen admitted that he had been jealous, that he was bothered by her staying with Jan.

And that had been true. He had actually been jealous. He had known that Jan was going to the same rehearsal as her, and when he woke up at four o'clock and she was not sleeping beside him, it occurred to him that she was perhaps sleeping somewhere else, with an Adonis from the railway, this *homo ludens* who had suddenly awakened her innermost desire. He had felt forsaken, and so afraid of losing her. Turid was pleased with his admissions. She maintained that it was unworthy of him to be jealous and that, in fact, it was also an insult to her. Nothing had happened, as he ought to have known. She had been having a deep conversation with Jan. The hours had flown by, because Jan had been telling her about his expectations of life, and she had been listening. She had been listening to a young man who still believed that life was really something that should be lived somewhere wholly different from here, in places where he wished he lived, and she had been so taken by the sudden openness of this man—who was so attractive and such a dreamer—that she had completely lost track of the time. If she had known it was so late and that Bjørn had woken up and felt tormented by such thoughts, she would have come home long ago. For some reason or other, Bjørn believed her, and afterward he always believed her assurances that there had been nothing going on.

For it happened that Turid Lammers began to come home in the early morning hours in much the same way, after a rehearsal which she (but not he) had attended, and it also happened that she very reluctantly broke away from a rehearsal they had both attended, or after a party, of which there were many in the circle around the Society, to return home with him because he wanted to leave (but not she), because she was all sparkle sitting in her stage outfit with some man, a genuine and self-important *homo ludens* who now, inspired by her presence, put on a performance in which he pushed himself to the limit, with a self-taught text conceived on the spur of the moment, which now collapsed, of course, since she had to get up and go home with her partner, because the Treasury opened at nine in the morning and for some incomprehensible reason everything would grind to a halt if the treasurer hadn't had enough sleep, the number of hours determined arbitrarily by the treasurer himself. Incomprehensible. Kongsberg Secondary School, after all, continued to function even if Miss Lammers went straight to her teacher's desk from a party at the Society, a fact sufficiently proven by the diplomas awarded to her pupils. Well, even the florist's shop of the Lammers sisters opened punctually at nine in the morning, and the saleswomen would, as a matter of fact, all be there, and the customers would not stay away even if the youngest Lammers sister had danced through the night, until the crack of dawn, instead of having been suddenly interrupted and dragged home by a jealous partner. On such occasions Bjørn Hansen walked beside her, as stiff as a poker. But he believed her assurances that his fear of losing her was completely groundless.

Why, then, did he get jealous? Why did he walk home from a party as stiff as a poker beside her? Why did he sometimes tremble with suppressed fury once the members of the merry Theater Society had left the Lammers villa after a party, and scream out his real message to her, his feeling that now he had lost her, forever? It happened time and again. Turid Lammers as a dazzling focal point. The circle lost in admiration around her. Among them her partner, Bjørn Hansen. That Turid was at the center of things did not mean that she sat in the middle, quite the contrary, because part of Turid Lammers's charm was also her modesty. Not only did she leave the principal roles to others, she also left the geometrical midpoint to others; she herself felt happiest at the small tables on the periphery, where she was first surrounded by both men and women, then by three or, alternatively, two men, until finally she was alone with one man, who immediately launched into his self-taught script as if for the first time—a teacher educated at Eik Teachers College who was now performing the scintillating script of how he had been cast under a spell in the mountainous Kongsberg area, because at long last he had acquired the sort of audience every amateur actor desires for his monologue, ever ready to be delivered: two starry eyes, waiting lips, a woman with French gestures, at once distant and approachable, and he did not notice that this secret monologue, to be privately performed for her alone, at a discreet side table, turned into a crowd scene in which he, as the lone walk-on, represented them all, on their knees in front of the admired Turid Lammers. Wasn't everyone now casting sidelong glances at Bjørn

Hansen? No, as the years went by, only new members shot sidelong glances his way, at first. But not later. For everyone learned that Turid Lammers was faithful to her Bjørn, which didn't lessen their admiration for her, at the same time as she let herself be unrestrainedly admired, even conquered, by a chosen one who sat spellbound at her table, although even he knew that he would in the end get up and go home, alone. (Or, if not, at any rate sleep alone, for Turid Lammers always left the chosen one's house or flat or rented room without allowing herself to be kissed passionately, but at most gently and sweetly, as she sometimes admitted openly to Bjørn, although the whole night might pass before that happened.) And Bjørn Hansen knew this. Which was why he could maintain his mask. But no sooner had the Society's members left the house than he blew his top, allowing all his jealousy to emerge. Turid Lammers thought so anyway. In reality it was nothing but a pretence on his part. He did it for her sake.

For he did not dare entertain the thought that Turid might display all of her feminine charm vis-à-vis the evening's chosen member of the Society without her partner becoming beside himself with jealousy. He could not bear the thought of causing her so much pain. Because what would happen then? Well, after Jan has been courting her for three hours, he gets up and leaves, together with the other guests. She is alone. Her husband is reading a novel in an adjacent room and now he comes to her and asks in a friendly voice, "Would you like a cup of tea?" Then he might as well have packed his belongings and moved. Out of the Lammers villa. Away from Kongsberg. What bound them to one another would have been lost.

So Bjørn Hansen watched his beloved. His mind darkened

by jealousy, he watched her as she sat chatting with Deputy Judge Stabenfeldt or the theater-mad Per Brønnum, who was a regular worker she flirted with for a while, and with whom she also spent hours at night in her coquettish way in his condemned flat in the center of Old Kongsberg. But actually Bjørn didn't care. He didn't believe that Turid Lammers was cheating on him—couldn't, in fact, picture it to himself in his wildest dreams; if she did, she would have told him straight out.

Yet he would have fits of jealousy, in which he showed her all the classic signs. And he was not just pretending, but felt the dark recesses of jealousy inside himself—a deep sense of being forsaken and a dark rage, repulsion and rejection, all of which streamed through him, darkly and deeply and quiveringly. But it was only playacting. He was observing himself coldly all the time as he paced the floor, showering her in his despair with accusations that she accepted with a show of emotion. This was his way of keeping her afloat. His way of worshipping the very ground she trod on.

That is, he was in the know. He knew what he was doing. He had made up his mind to live with Turid Lammers at Kongsberg. As the Kongsberg town treasurer. In his leisure time he was involved in amateur theater. His love for her was so great that he could have gone mad out of jealousy. Had he not renounced everything in order to cultivate the temptation in all its intensity, for what was left, after all, except this intensity? But he was in the know. He knew what he was doing. He fully realized that, after living with Turid for seven years, his chief contribution to preserving their relationship consisted in these outbursts of fake jealousy. He had seen through her. He had no illusions about her.

Life. He had lived with Turid Lammers for seven years and soon would be forty, a middle-aged man. What had he got out of his life? He was the town treasurer at Kongsberg, which was something. He had become convinced that he possessed some talent as an amateur actor, and for six evenings in the autumn he trod the boards at the Kongsberg Cinema and felt the joy of it. Oh yes, he felt the joy of it. It was a strange, deep feeling. After seven years as Turid Lammers's partner in the Lammers villa he knew everything about the joy of intoning, along with two teachers and Dr. Schiøtz at the hospital, the same stanza at exactly the same time, in precisely the same tone of voice, while all four of them stamped their left feet on the floor with exactly the same force in precisely the same moment in the heated atmosphere of the stage of the Kongsberg Cinema, standing in the spotlight and before the compact public in the darkness out there, down there. A shudder through your body, the sensual pleasure of the precision. In the dark out there, those thousand mouths, those two thousand eyes hidden in the dark watching them all, including the four walk-ons, who were showing what they were capable of. Yes, he really liked it, to step forward in this way, in addition to helping to see through an entire production by being part of a team. But was it really life? This was what Bjørn Hansen asked himself as he more and more often sought refuge among his books, where he could breathe, and brood. Who was Turid Lammers? She saw that Bjørn Hansen was asking himself questions and burning the midnight oil, and she wanted to share his books but noticed that he was not particularly eager to do so. She, too, was approaching forty, but she was still capable of twisting a man round her little finger, as they say. He kept an eye on her.

While he constantly watched over her and kept up his jealousy, he contemplated her. She was the natural center of the Kongsberg Theater Society, an association of enthusiasts who filled their lives by laboriously setting up and carrying through six performances a year of some of the most popular operettas of our time. In full public view. On the stage. In the limelight. For seven years Bjørn Hansen had been one of these enthusiasts. Treasurer in the day, enthusiast in the evening. Was that enough? Could there not be more? Bjørn Hansen was going on forty, and he screamed for something more. He began to throw out hints that perhaps they should try for something big. All this enthusiasm, all this experience of how to conduct oneself on the stage, all this delight in precision and in displaying one's abilities—couldn't it be used for something more than performing operettas, which, while capable of kindling a gaiety of spirit both in the actors and, not least, in the public, could nevertheless make one feel rather dejected, or outright weary, with all their intellectual vacuity, everything considered, after the lights had come up in the hall, the public had gone home, and they sat in the dressing room removing their makeup? What if they rose to a level where one could feel the blast of real life? What if they had a shot at Ibsen?

For two years Bjørn Hansen kept hinting that they should have a shot at Ibsen. It evoked little response. In particular, his effort to arouse their enthusiasm by pointing out the feelings of emptiness they were left with once a performance was over, due to an operetta's lack of intellectual substance, cut no ice. It was an attack on everything they stood for, and it was foolish on Bjørn Hansen's part to call attention to it, although they had certainly felt this dejection, some of them in any case.

However, he was supported by two of the Society's members, and they were not just anybody. One of them was the singing dentist, Herman Busk.

Herman Busk had an exceptionally fine baritone voice, which many thought was fit to be heard on more important stages than the one in the Kongsberg Cinema six times a year. He was one of the guiding spirits of the Society, and if he did not take the lead, he had in any case the next most important male role. But it was at rehearsals that he was most impressive, usually outside the program. How many times had the others packed up, about to leave, when Herman Busk suddenly began to sing the melody they had heard him rehearse all evening. Everything was in place. All of his painstaking practice had suddenly produced results, and they listened spellbound, all of them thinking, "This will be a stunning number on stage." As it turned out to be, although perhaps falling short of their predictions. Maybe the expectations were too great; Herman Busk never reached the truly great heights on the stage proper—he was good enough to brilliantly defend his moniker "The Singing Dentist," but not to fulfill the expectations that had been awakened in those cramped rehearsal rooms with one's hand on the door, about to step out into the evening darkness and the deserted streets. Now, however, Herman Busk became interested in the Society doing Ibsen, and Bjørn Hansen's idea could no longer be dismissed. Incidentally, due to this surprising stand, Herman Busk and Bjørn Hansen became better acquainted with one another; they would sit and discuss things for hours and became intimate friends—indeed, Bjørn Hansen came to look upon Herman Busk as his best friend.

The other person who backed him was Turid Lammers. That was a surprise, for Turid had no relationship to Ibsen. She spoke nicely about him, of course, and treated him as a classic, but she did not care very much for his plays. This he knew because they had seen Ibsen performances at the National Theater in the capital several times, but these she had suffered in silence. So that she might now actively work to have her own dear Theater Society put on *The Wild Duck* was unbelievable to him. In reality she did not care about operettas either, as a spectator. It was too banal fare for her, despite everything; true, she was eager for them to go to Oslo when the Norwegian Theater put on one of its annual musicals, but that was simply to pick up a few tricks. Still, operettas were what she felt closest to. Originally he had thought that her kind of theater would be avant-garde, as it had been when he was her lover as a married man in Oslo, but when she moved back to Kongsberg with its Theater Society, it was all operettas and there was no more talk about avant-garde theater; in some way, however, avant-garde theater and operettas had one thing in common for her, namely, that the content signified nothing, the masquerade everything. What she had been absorbed by in avant-garde theater were the masks and nothing else. They had no children together. Turid Lammers did not become a mother; she would sometimes allude flirtatiously to her not having children, calling it the tragedy of her life. But actually Turid Lammers did not want children, she was not prepared for that. Not now. If she were to have had children, she would have had them with her first husband, in France, in the 1960s, and Bjørn could have pictured to himself her leaving France head over heels, holding a small child on her arm as she waited at Gare du Nord for the night train to Copenhagen (and from there to Oslo) to be set up. But when she came back to Oslo after seven years in Paris, it was without a child. As a solitary woman, free, restless, who took a lover, a man to whom she later bound herself and took with her when she returned to the town of her childhood. Turid Lammers was childless and wanted to remain childless—in her innermost self she wanted to be the last. Operettas were to her a brilliant pretext to carry into effect what to Turid Lammers was theater: costumes, masks, wigs, quick changes, pace, pace. But now she supported her partner's idea that the Kongsberg Theater Society should stage *The Wild Duck* by Henrik Ibsen, and very actively at that. Was it to show her loyalty? Toward him and toward the others? Did she want to present herself as Bjørn Hansen's loyal partner, willing to fight in order for him to realize this plan that he felt so passionately about, and which she too felt passionately about now, since it was his plan, although everyone understood that in reality she didn't care a damn, except for the fact that her partner happened to feel so passionately that the Society should stage something which would give them all a lift, *The Wild Duck* by Henrik Ibsen.

That is to say, Turid Lammers's support was a handsome gesture, a mark of favor from the circle's central figure to her rather anonymous husband when, for once, he needed it. But while respect for Turid Lammers increased, as an argument for staging *The Wild Duck* by Henrik Ibsen her support proved counterproductive. Why go overboard? Just because Turid Lammers's partner had taken it into his head that they should aspire to something higher, were they to put on a play for which they simply lacked the qualifications to succeed? This was what was muttered in the corners, but since a mainstay like Herman Busk was in favor of it, besides a number of others who were also familiar with the sense of emptiness that a successful operetta performance could leave in their minds once the curtain had gone down, and who could also easily imagine, for once, trying to reach for the impossible, it was decided that the Society's next production would be *The Wild Duck* by Henrik Ibsen.

And when Turid Lammers proposed that Bjørn Hansen himself should appear in the role of Hjalmar Ekdal, nobody protested. Apart from Bjørn Hansen. He had not meant to reserve the lead for himself, that was not why he had made his proposal; it had never occurred to him. But his protests, which were quite mild anyway, were simply dismissed—of course, Bjørn Hansen would appear as Hjalmar Ekdal. Many supported him simply because it meant that he would be nailed to the imminent fiasco, made to feel it in the flesh, up on the stage, while it was taking place. This he understood, and that was why he accepted the assignment. The great role of Gregers Werle was intended for Herman Busk, but the singing dentist refused. Too big a part for him, he claimed. On the other hand, he could very well be Old Ekdal, unless they found someone who was better qualified. And so Brian Smith was chosen to be Gregers Werle. With his broken Norwegian this English engineer from the Kongsberg Arms Factory would give a new dimension to the uncompromising merchant's son from Ibsen's world of ideas. Dr. Schiøtz would play Dr. Relling. This, too, was proposed by Turid Lammers, and it was obviously an attempt at wooing the public. A physician at the Kongsberg Hospital appears in the part of a physician in a play—one of

Henrik Ibsen's at that. Dr. Schiøtz as Dr. Relling, the besotted physician with his clear-sightedness. But Dr. Schiøtz refused. Turid put all her charm into persuading him, but Dr. Schiøtz refused. Who was Dr. Schiøtz? No one knew. He was one of the more serious and unapproachable among the group of *homo ludens* types that made up the Kongsberg Theater Society. A man in a doctor's smock, tall and thin. With sensitive fingers—a pianist? Not as far as they knew, but he was a cross-country skier. During the winter months he was seen early in the morning up in the hills around the town, going at full speed along the plateaus on his racing skis. In the theater he always played walk-on parts, swapping duties at the hospital in order to appear in the background, as Mr. Nobody, in all those operettas. But he refused to be Dr. Relling. The woman who was chosen for the part of Hedvig, however, did not say no. For that role a twenty-one-year-old nursing student was an obvious choice, not least because she had such a sweet and childish face. Turid Lammers also made it into the cast. She was to play Hjalmar Ekdal's wife and Hedvig's mother: Gina Ekdal.

The theater director hailed from the capital; it was common practice to hire directors from outside, so there were plenty of them roaming all around the country, staging operettas and farces for local amateur theaters. But tracking down an itinerant Ibsen director was not easy. Finally they found an unemployed director in Oslo. He came up, attended the rehearsals, drank steadily, and can scarcely have remembered anything of it all. On the other hand, Hjalmar Ekdal (aka Bjørn Hansen) did.

To make a long story very short: it turned out to be a total flop. It was an extremely poor performance, and the scheduled six showings were reduced to four, the fourth and last of which had eighteen paying spectators in the auditorium. True, the director was a has-been, and drunk to boot, but Bjørn Hansen knew that they could not put the blame on him; he was simply an illustration of how things were, and how they had been all along. They just couldn't pull it off. Bjørn Hansen had carefully studied Ibsen's play, with underlinings, and thought he had understood it so thoroughly that he felt Hjalmar Ekdal's *Weltschmerz* in himself. But to no avail. He knew how it should be done, of course, but in practice it became something quite different from what he had imagined. It became clunky. Oh, this naivete of Hjalmar Ekdal, which Bjørn Hansen knew and thought he had made his own—he would defend it and act it out as it had never been acted out before, because it arose from such a deep pain that he could not bear looking truth in the face, his smallness being based on the fact that he found himself in a great tragedy, which had befallen him through no fault of his own. But none of this emerged from Bjørn Hansen. None of this was part of his physical presence on the stage. It did not work. It turned into mere talk. He was nothing but a glum and tedious body on a stage. He made his gestures to no avail. Like the others. Like Gregers Werle, like Old Ekdal, like Hedvig, little Hedvig, whom Hjalmar Ekdal loved so deeply that he could not bear seeing her any more. Bjørn Hansen stood on stage acting a part, rather stupidly, as even he himself thought. The public did not laugh him to scorn, oh no, they tried to encourage him by showing their interest, by not yawning—well, even with tepid applause. But it was not up to scratch.

They couldn't do it. It was all too clear that this was something for which they lacked every qualification. Bjørn Hansen had insufficient radiance to enable him to make Hjalmar Ekdal's painful gestures. That was the bitter truth. He had not enough acting technique, and hence no radiance. It is not enough to feel, inwardly. That was demonstrated at the Kongsberg Cinema four times in the late autumn of 1983 (wasn't it?).

And he had known it all along. He had known it was impossible, nobody can say otherwise. He knew that much about acting, about its being a profession, about art being involved, etc., that he realized he couldn't possibly create the illusion of being Hjalmar Ekdal. But his desire to do so had been so damn strong that he had been unable to even consider this obvious fact.

This also applied to the others. Neither individually nor as an acting ensemble did they have what it took to perform this world-class play. If Hjalmar Ekdal was tedious on stage, the English engineer Brian Smith was no better as Gregers Werle, and his broken Norwegian by no means elevated his exchanges with Hjalmar Ekdal, in fact quite the contrary, and little Hedvig, who may have been sweet, was unfortunately unable to breathe life into the fragile figure who entered the attic and was so theatrical that Hjalmar Ekdal went rigid with terror during those sensitive moments when they had the large, empty stage entirely to themselves.

Afterward they were both equally unhappy. The other actors took their defeat with composure, Bjørn Hansen and little Hedvig being the only ones who mourned—Bjørn Hansen in spite of knowing that the big effort he had spoken so fervently of for two years had been impossible for obvious reasons. It had been different with little Hedvig, who had thought it was possible. She was twenty-one, in her second year at the Drammen Nursing School; she had taken the train to Kongsberg for the rehearsals every afternoon, and had then waited at the station to take the last train back to her rented room in Drammen afterward. What they did not know until later, when it came to light, was that she had taken six months' leave from the Nursing School and used her student loan of 15,000 kroner to get to know Hedvig's soul. With disastrous results. Although she had been fascinated by this invented fourteen-year-old girl's mind—probably because it revealed to her a number of deep things about herself, which she had not been able to convey to anyone, not even her best friend, being so far removed from everyday speech as they were, but which she now discovered touched her in a fundamental way, and had a bearing on her quite frictionless relationship to her own parents—she managed nonetheless to destroy everything by acting in an appallingly stagey manner, and she did not even understand what was wrong, only that it was, and she wept on Hjalmar Ekdal's grief-stricken shoulders after every one of those four performances. She had continued to live in a furnished room in Drammen, both during the rehearsals and the performances, because she had not dared admit to her parents, who lived in Kongsberg, in a house where her own room was always ready, how much she had really staked on becoming nothing less than inspired by appearing as Hedvig in *The Wild Duck* by Henrik Ibsen. And therefore she had dutifully gone back to Drammen and her alleged nurse's training after each performance, also after the first night and before the first-night party.

While little Hedvig wept on Bjørn Hansen's shoulder in the dressing room after the curtain came down the first night,

Gina Ekdal came in, radiant. Gina Ekdal (aka Turid Lammers) had reasons to be radiant, because she was the only one who had salvaged something out of the wreck of this performance, one might say. Seeing the grief-stricken Bjørn Hansen and the weeping Hedvig, she said, "But it went all right, after all, with curtain calls and everything," without her forced encouragement helping at all. But for her the performance had been a success; she had taken the public by storm. It made her elated, and she barely noticed that a twenty-one-year-old sweet young woman was resting her head on her partner's shoulder, for the other actors and the stage crew flocked round her, complimenting her on her acting, which had saved the whole evening, without at all considering that what had saved the evening and made her a success was that she had quite simply betrayed the entire performance by doing her act at cross-purposes to the ensemble. Turid Lammers had been fully aware that she was to represent a female character in an Ibsen play who possibly harbored a somber secret that caused everything to fall apart, for others. She had loyally tried to bring out the serious nature of Gina Ekdal's life and secret, without achieving anything but superficiality, and in this perspective she was no better or worse than the rest of the ensemble. But after noticing the lack of response from the audience, she broke away, conferring upon her character a charm that made the public wake up and chuckle with satisfaction. Turid played Gina Ekdal with overdone gestures, with cheap tricks, oh, she wagged her tail and charmed the local audience, which willingly succumbed to her for a fleeting moment.

Bjørn Hansen stood there with his tedious Hjalmar Ekdal witnessing all this. Onstage. With Gina Ekdal. The two of them were the only ones there. In the next to last scene. Now, too, when the fiasco was obvious, he yearned to portray this ridiculous figure, Hjalmar Ekdal, for he knew that this character was profoundly tragic, and this had to be made clear. Hjalmar Ekdal was a key that opened the door to some really dizzying questions; his fate had to be enacted in such a way that he could really hold his own against Gregers Werle's last words to the effect that, if he now, after Hedvig's death in the final scene, was capable of producing nothing but empty rhetoric, then life was simply not worth living—something that now, when Bjørn Hansen tried to bring out their meaning, fell flat. And there, beside him, was Gina Ekdal in the figure of Turid Lammers, radiant. He went down, but she refused to go down with him. Instead she wagged her tail and for a fleeting moment the audience forgot about this untalented production and allowed itself to be seduced by Turid Lammers. She stole the scene. Bjørn Hansen bravely played on as he approached the end of his project, while Turid displayed all of her charms. She stood there, in the merciful spotlight, a thick layer of makeup on her face, elated at having taken the public by storm, trembling all over, in fact, as Bjørn Hansen, who stood very close, could clearly see. Turid betrayed everything. The whole idea behind the performance, and behind him, in order to save what could be saved. Turid Lammers's charm was to overpower Bjørn Hansen's unsuccessful seriousness. It was a violation of everything they had agreed on in advance, and Bjørn Hansen ought to have felt a pinch of surprise at being stabbed in the back in this way. He should have accused her, asking with a deep groan as this was going on: "Why, why are you doing this to me?" But he did not. He did not ask himself why she acted as she did. He only felt relief. Not because she was trying to salvage something from the wreckage, but because she refused to go down with him.

In truth, he had been ill at ease with her eager support of his project to undertake this big effort. There was something about her loyalty that had a suffocating effect on him. It bound her to him at a time when Bjørn Hansen was about to break away. Because Turid Lammers had faded. She had turned forty-four, and it had long been clear that the ravages of the years had left their mark on her face and body. Her face had become sharp, scraped, hard. How he missed the softness of it! But that was gone forever, and along with it many of the ideas on which Bjørn Hansen had built his whole way of life. He had made his home here. At Kongsberg. Alongside Turid Lammers. He had left everything behind, because he was afraid he would regret it all his life if he chose not to pursue the temptation that emanated from her body and face. Now this face and this body offered nothing but memories of something that had been lost forever, making the whole situation unendurable. He had suspected this for a long time.

Turid Lammers was still the natural center of her and Bjørn Hansen's milieu. The circle around the Kongsberg Theater Society was fairly close, and its core consisted on the whole of the same individuals as when Bjørn Hansen had moved here twelve years ago, though there had been a few changes. Some had dropped out, others had joined. Like the old-timers, the new members also learned to treat Turid Lammers as the natural center. But she was so in a different way than before, both to the veterans, whether they realized it or not, and to the new arrivals. They constantly crowded around her table, which was still placed slightly off center, but whereas these meetings always used to end with one man sitting alone with her, in a (to him) dizzying tête-à-tête—although he (and the others) knew it meant nothing except that he was sitting there at that moment and couldn't hope for anything to happen, yet found it to be enough, yes, enough—now when Bjørn Hansen showed up to suggest that they should go home, there were occasionally two or three gentlemen at her table, engaged in relaxed and cheerful conversation, sometimes also other groupings, like one man and two women (besides Turid), or two men and two women, etc., etc. And while previously the men had *looked* at her, now they were content to talk about her, albeit with great admiration. Well, they also spoke directly to her, with open admiration for what she stood for, what she was, and for the importance of what she was doing, and not least for what she had done for the Kongsberg Theater Society. They showered her with compliments, both men and women, old and new members. They also addressed themselves to Bjørn Hansen, her life partner. They let Bjørn Hansen know what a ravishing woman Turid Lammers was. What enthusiasm! What daring! At the outset Bjørn Hansen felt slightly bewildered as he looked into the honest eyes of a thirty-year-old engineer who had just let him know what a ravishing woman Turid Lammers was. So capable! Some also said she was courageous. And fun. And how youthful she was, mentally. Bjørn Hansen had to stand listening to all of this, not without being struck by a terrible feeling of loneliness. Though they may not themselves have noticed, Bjørn Hansen understood that they were reacting to the established fact that the years had left their traces on his companion's face and that consequently they could speak about her in a manner that consigned her enchantment to a bygone chapter of her and the circle's history, and that it was nothing to make a fuss about. He felt abandoned by them. They were people at play, paying homage to Miss Lammers, praising her for her hairdo, her pretty dresses, her importance to the milieu, to maintaining solidarity and enthusiasm, but they did so with a light touch, playfully light. This in spite of having discovered that she had faded. But it did not matter to them; the years pass, as we all know, and with a shrug they left it to Bjørn Hansen to live with her from day to day, now as before.

And Turid behaved as before. She was the same as ever. Made the same well-known acquired French gestures and was still able to draw a man irresistibly to her with her eyes, to be with him now, in the present moment, the two of them only. She was far from without charm and still knew the basic rules of how to attract a man's attention. But no man was as interested as before in being attracted. If he belonged to the old innermost core, he appeared to join in the game, but grew theatrical, producing a comical, if not pathetic effect. The new men felt embarrassed. They had learned to respect her as an outstanding drama teacher, but they did not know how to react to her unaffected, ingratiating manner, having the effect of an invitation, which in the past they would not have been able to tear themselves away from to save their lives. Previously everyone had known that Turid Lammers, although she flirted, never gave way and remained faithful (to Bjørn), but all the same they found her so attractive that they acted toward her as if they were in the midst of their life's adventure. Now, however, the new men's suspicion was aroused when she flirted. They actually believed that she was coming on to them and tried to make their getaway. Bjørn Hansen had observed this time and again. Even at home, in the Lammers villa. Turid Lammers had always dragged men home to rehearse songs. Bjørn Hansen would come home from the Treasury in the afternoon and hear charming operetta melodies through the door of the room with the piano in it, then enter to find Turid Lammers with a male member of the Society. Now as before he could see how coquettishly Turid Lammers behaved, with her attempts at direct eye contact, at closeness—by, for example, patting the man lovingly on the sleeve of his jacket to achieve intimacy, an old trick she had, or a habit—but now the years had gone by and, radiant with joy, the thirty-year-old engineer welcomed Bjørn Hansen as his rescuer, gushed about how much theater meant to him, to his self-realization in a hard and materialistic world of computers, grabbed his sheet music from the stand on the piano and rushed out of the door. Bjørn Hansen was left standing there, helpless, alone with his Turid. How he would have wished that this engineer had been so engrossed by Turid Lammers as she sat before the piano, tossing her head back as she looked him straight in the face, that, still bewildered and ecstatic because she had lightly brushed the sleeve of his jacket with her fingers, he had not realized that he, Bjørn Hansen, had entered the room—or, if he had noticed, had pretended not to have noticed in order to savor his last few stolen moments with this woman! If he had done so, Bjørn Hansen would not now have stood there so terribly lonely with Turid Lammers, seeing clearly how her small double chin, her distinct wrinkles, and the dry skin of her formerly soft arms had removed her for good from him. And Turid? Did she not understand? That it was over for good? She must have understood, but she did not turn a hair. Even when a thirty-year-old engineer, who felt the greatest enthusiasm for her as a drama teacher, rushed out of the door, gratefully seizing the opportunity to dash off, she did not turn a hair. True enough, they both felt a bit embarrassed, but they acted as if nothing had happened. What could they do? Turid Lammers chose to act as before. As the center. It was actually easy for her, because in these twelve years she had, after all, had one man only, namely him, Bjørn Hansen. Was that why she suddenly, and so surprisingly, supported him when he wanted Kongsberg's avatars of *homo ludens* to perform Ibsen instead of musicals? She must have suspected that he had long ago given up every idea of belonging to a circle of *homo ludens* types, and that the sense of estrangement he felt at being in a chorus and singing operetta tunes had become so great that he wanted to break with the illusion, which had lasted for more than a decade of his one and only life. He knew that his proposal, if it were carried out and went well, would mean that the Kongsberg Theater Society would be divided between those who wanted to continue with what Bjørn Hansen had called "big efforts" and those who would like to continue to express themselves rhythmically and musically, in an everlastingly popular vein. She absolutely preferred the latter, but she sided with Bjørn and went in for Ibsen. While she acted just as before, as a center, though conscious of the fact that it was over. After all, she looked at her face without makeup in the mirror every morning. Was that why she constantly returned to the notion, vis-à-vis other women, that she had never felt as young as now, because when she was young she had lacked the courage to be young, and, vis-à-vis Bjørn and other men, that, inside, she was still a young girl? He was supported, that is, by a woman who maintained, like a magic incantation, that she was still a young girl inside, although, Bjørn thought (brutally, he thought), this was obvious to nobody any more. Perhaps she believed one could sense it from her movements, which were still vigorous, due to lots of training and skill (but quite without grace); if measured against grace, they failed and became the shrill and pathetic movements that a woman in her forties makes in order to imitate her lost youth—could she not see that? Or regarding her fictitious longings when she patted the sleeve of a man's jacket just as she had done in the springtime of her life, must not the man conclude from the gesture to its source, she no doubt thought, though of no avail, a no avail, however, that she could not accept. But she realized she had lost. Therefore she supported Bjørn Hansen. But it was too late. He was glad, of course, to have her support, because it obviously increased the chances that his idea of the big effort might be realized, but also because it hinted that their relationship could continue, calmly and resignedly, grounded in loyalty and not in the beauty we pursue—well, he tried to see it like that in any case. But at the same time he also saw the other thing. His terrible loneliness living with a faded beauty. A woman the others gladly left to him, after showering her with noncommittal, though sincere, compliments. It's good we have Turid, they must have thought, and good we have Bjørn, who has undertaken to live with her, right close to her. Bjørn Hansen was bothered by the hard features of Turid's face, the taut lines, without softness, which were accompanied to excess by a glaringly contrasting sudden cry or peep: "I'm still a young girl inside, I've never been as young as now," which made a thirty-year-old engineer wash his hands of them and, relieved, rush out of the door when Bjørn turned up at last and could carry out his matrimonial obligation, take care of her, keep her for himself, so that he, the engineer, with his whole life ahead of him, could rush out of the door, liberated from the terrible prospect of ending up in her withered arms, the arms in which Bjørn Hansen still found himself, because of events that had taken place twelve years ago.

Her unfailing loyalty bound him to her. He experienced it as a clinch, but could do nothing about it. And he was glad to have her support, albeit suspicious. And when Turid continued so ardently to support the idea that the Kongsberg Theater Society should really undertake the bold effort of staging Ibsen and then, during the rehearsals, eagerly worked at the role of Gina Ekdal, without any trace of glamour or festivity, his suspicion ceased. He now envisaged a collaboration, well, a camaraderie between them, which could become sufficiently deep to still the pain of awakening by her side in the morning and seeing her haggard face, without makeup. Indeed, he saw that she counted on it, saw it with his own eyes. Therefore he, too, decided to try. A life in seriousness and camaraderie within the framework of an amateur theater society, the avatars of *homo ludens* in the godforsaken provincial town of Kongsberg, where they would attempt a truly big effort. Until it turned out that the project itself did not work (and could never work), he could, in his marriage to Turid Lammers, discern the contours of an uncomplaining mature life, which did not tempt him, but which could ease the pain of that other thing, the unbearable sight, and the realization that his whole life had been a pursuit of something that was destined to dissolve, because Nature has no mercy. He was glad to have Turid Lammers's resigned, unfailing loyalty, which she offered with her exceptional and practiced charm. But in reality he wanted to get away. That was what he wanted. He knew he could not ease the pain. But he was chained to her.

Then she did it, broke away, betraying him openly on the stage under the pretext of picking up the pieces of an amateur production. Was it worth it? Did she know what she was doing? How elated Turid was in that fateful moment! Her whole body trembled. Which only Bjørn Hansen (aka the tedious Hjalmar Ekdal) could notice, because he stood so close to her on the stage. Those quivering knees, that face touched with emotion, scenting the public's favor for a fleeting moment. Turned inward, moved, she was swathed in her own cheap success—this was Turid Lammers, excited, intoxicated, at any price. This was her pleasure. Bjørn Hansen was liberated from her at last. He knew in her moment of glory that he would no longer live with her at any price. Nevertheless, two years went by before the final break. Because what was he to tell her? That he felt life had passed him by because he no longer found her face and body attractive? That he was unable to reconcile himself to the fact that her soft beauty had abandoned her forever, leaving behind a woman for whom he felt nothing as she lay beside him in bed? For a man to see his wife in that way is unbearable and strikes him dumb. And so he remains stuck with her. The two years that went by before he managed to tear himself away from her were a total nightmare, which here will be passed over in silence.

Eventually he packed his earthly belongings and moved into a flat in a modern block in the center of Kongsberg. By himself at last. He could catch his breath, walk about in his own living room and enjoy a quiet life. His flat was on the third floor; from the balcony he could see the railway station right below, to the left. The building and the tracks, which soon vanished from his sight as they merged into one, both in the north and south, circling Kongsberg in an attractive arc. In a way, Kongsberg was fenced in by the railway track, with the express passenger trains on their way to Kristiansand and Stavanger in one direction, Oslo in the other. Every evening just before midnight, the night train to Kristiansand and Stavanger stopped at the station. The train with its lowered window shades, the stillness. Not a sound coming from the station then, as opposed to when the trains stopped during the day and their arrivals were announced over the loudspeaker, which could be clearly heard in Bjørn Hansen's living room, even on Sundays. From his balcony he could see, on the right, a corner of the river that flowed through the town. The river was called Lågen, and since its source was located far up on the Numedal plateaus, it was called Numedalslågen. Kongsberg is situated far inland, but Numedalslågen, which runs through the town, continues to flow, in zigzags and curves, mile after mile, until it finally reaches the coast at Larvik. The part Bjørn Hansen could see was quite peculiar, for right there sat three minuscule islands covered with tall pine trees, a sight that Bjørn Hansen liked very much, though most of all he would have wanted to see one of the many waterfalls Numedalslågen forms where it passes Kongsberg, forming another attractive arc. The arc the river makes is particularly attractive where it passes Old Kongsberg, with its seventeenth-century church, on a height, and the silhouette of three or four magnificent patrician buildings from the end of the eighteenth century. That view looked exceptionally good from up on the railway bridge, which had a pedestrian walkway beside the railway tracks that Bjørn Hansen was in the habit of including in his Sunday stroll, almost regardless of where else he had decided to go. Then, too, he could bend over the rusty barbed wire fence and look down on the river, at the black water, and study its reflections and ripples.

Incidentally, Bjørn Hansen would often take these Sunday walks with Herman Busk, the singing dentist. They tramped about in Kongsbergmarka, in the hills above the city, where they walked paths that led up to the peaks, to the popular Knutehytta, for example. They were both dressed in knickerbockers and anoraks, in the old-fashioned style, as they loafed about in the open and talked together. They were both middle-aged men, respected by the society in which they had long ago found their place. Herman Busk as dentist, Bjørn Hansen as treasurer. Sunday was the day for outings. Crowds of people on the paths in the hills above the old silver-mining town. Hikers. Both Bjørn Hansen and Herman Busk would constantly meet people they greeted before going on, or stopped to exchange a few words with, either Herman Busk or Bjørn Hansen, while the other remained standing alongside. They might be mutual acquaintances from the Society or people Bjørn Hansen knew from his occupation as treasurer, or clients of Herman Busk. When they returned to the town after their tramp, they would often go to Herman Busk's house, where Mrs. Busk awaited them with Sunday dinner. Or they parted company and went each to his own place. It was once a month or so that Bjørn Hansen was invited for Sunday dinner with the Busk family. He appreciated that, for nothing could be compared to returning from a long ramble in field and forest, entering the hallway of Herman Busk's residence, and feeling the fragrance of the Sunday roast tickle one's nostrils, as Bjørn Hansen also loudly proclaimed, in a way that delighted Herman Busk's wife, Berit. But he made no fuss about dining alone either. On Sundays it happened quite frequently that he dined at the Grand Hotel, because its restaurant had an excellent kitchen, better than the old Kongsberg Pub, which had not regained its old-time excellence since its renovation after a fire some years ago. He liked to dine in restaurants on Sundays, alone, served by a polite waiter who knew him because he ate there so often. Then Bjørn Hansen would often sit and reflect on what he and Herman Busk had talked about while hiking along the paths in the heights above the town. They discussed a good amount of literature, because both of them were great readers. True, their tastes differed considerably, Herman preferring bulky, rather conventional novels, normally published by the Book Club, while Bjørn Hansen on the whole bought his books at the book dealers' annual giant sale, where the real goodies could be found. Therefore they could only seldom profitably discuss individual works, since Herman Busk had not read the books Bjørn Hansen had read, and Bjørn Hansen did not care for the books Herman Busk was reading. But he liked to listen to Herman Busk telling him about them, not least about why he appreciated them, perhaps not so much on account of the arguments or words he used, but because of the tone of voice, which indicated that they had a common frame of reference, even though both were alone vis-à-vis the other in regard to the great reading experiences they had within this common frame of reference. For the same reason Bjørn Hansen knew that Herman Busk understood him when he could proudly announce late one Sunday in the autumn as the trees were shedding their leaves and the paths were covered with yellow foliage, like a carpet (or like trash, if you preferred to see it that way), that now Camilo José Cela had received the Nobel Prize in Literature, for he had read a novel by Cela called *The Family of Pascual Duarte*. He had found it at the giant sale seven years ago, a single copy, which he alone had been interested in, though he got it for a song. Not many people in Norway had heard of Camilo José Cela, and no more than a couple of hundred copies were likely to have been sold, even though it had been available at the giant sale, and he was thus one of the two hundred. From interviews that Bjørn Hansen had read after Cela received the prize, he understood that few of the literary big shots who were interviewed had read anything by him. But one man at Kongsberg did know about him. The town treasurer at Kongsberg had discovered this novel, which had been spun from the head of a Spanish author of the highest quality, and that was something, eh? Where were the other two hundred readers? There must be several in our three largest cities, Oslo, Bergen and Trondheim, and among the two hundred there were most likely also Spanish-speaking individuals scattered about the far-flung country who had read it in Norwegian to check the translation, but if one could undertake an exact survey one would no doubt be in for a surprise. There was this one person at Kongsberg anyway, but Bjørn Hansen was certain that, in some little village or other in Norway, there was a cluster of Cela readers, at Geithus, for example. Geithus? Why not? There might very well be fifteen Cela readers at Geithus, that was how things were—the reading of certain novels is like an epidemic in miniature, a secret epidemic that suddenly breaks out in the strangest places while leaving others unaffected. "It was not that way before, but that's how it is now," Bjørn Hansen said, talking excitedly because he was proud to be among the two hundred select members of the secret brotherhood that had read Camilo José Cela's novel *The Family of Pascual Duarte*. "A somber novel, by the way," Bjørn Hansen added, "it deals with an illiterate man who commits murder in cold blood; it's a Spanish legend that says something about how people grow up in the scorched and cracked Extremadura landscape in Spain. But," he added meditatively, "was it somber enough? I mean, I liked the book, but did it go deeply enough, I mean deeply enough into my own existence?" After saying this he fell silent, nor did Herman Busk know what to say. They walked in silence side by side. That was how it mostly was—Bjørn Hansen's tirade prompted by the award of the Nobel Prize to Cela being an exception rather than the rule; they tended to speak when they felt like it, often in such monologues, but mostly they walked side by side absorbed by their own thoughts, interrupted only when they had to return the friendly nods of passersby. At the time when Cela received the Nobel Prize, however, Bjørn Hansen had been more reticent than usual, because he had developed an affliction that bothered him. His teeth had begun to give him pain. He was not sure when they had begun to do so; his teeth may have bothered him for a long time already without his being aware of it, until lately, when he had to face the fact that he would soon be fifty, had reached the summit and was about to begin the downhill run. But he was really worried about his teeth, which ached, or throbbed dully at any rate. He felt like mentioning it to Herman Busk, but decided he would not trouble him. Once a year Busk, the dentist, summoned him to an annual examination and carefully checked his teeth. Apart from that, they never talked about it. But now his teeth had started to hurt and the next consultation must be nine months away. Bjørn Hansen was really worried, not so much because of the pain, which he could easily tolerate, but because of what it signified. He was afraid that the pain meant that his teeth were falling out, coming loose from the gums and falling straight out, one after the other. Every so often he had to make an effort not to confide in Herman Busk concerning his worries. And this despite the fact that he knew, at least believed, that Herman would be annoyed if he knew he was going about in such an anxious state of mind and still decided not to have a good talk with him, Herman Busk, who would have immediately given him an appointment on Monday. But it was probably nothing, thought Bjørn. It's just my imagination, it would be stupid to bother a friend with imaginary problems in his leisure time, he thought. And so they walked in silence beside one another on their hikes along the paths in Kongsbergmarka in the hills above the town. Interrupted by a remark or a long tirade. While Bjørn Hansen considered carefully, pro and con, whether or not to mention his worries about his teeth and, in the end, chose not to bother the dentist, he readily let his thoughts wander and his words flow on other matters, and then he would often say things that amazed Herman Busk. As when the town treasurer suddenly said that nearly all of the books he liked were merciless books that showed life to be impossible and contained a bitter black humor. In a way that was quite all right, revealing a side to his friend that Herman Busk recognized. But when he then added, "I'm getting tired of them now," and then explained this comment by adding that what he now wanted to read was a novel that showed life to be impossible, but without a trace of humor, black or otherwise, then Herman was taken aback and could think of nothing else to say aside from observing that there are certainly plenty of books without a trace of humor, whereupon Bjørn Hansen fell back and said he was damn right about that—"and they are all quite boring." But then they had reached town again and stepped out onto the old railway bridge, where they stood side by side leaning over the railing and staring down at the river below, before they continued along the walkway beside the railway track, turned off it to take a shortcut down into a densely built-up area and reached the street corner, where they either parted company and went their separate ways or proceeded together to Herman Busk's residence, where Berit was waiting with her Sunday roast.

Bjørn turned fifty. The day was celebrated quietly in his own company, in the splendid isolation of his flat in a Kongsberg tower block. He had made clear in advance that he did not wish any attention, and it was respected. He received an offer from *Aftenposten* to have the day noted there, if he sent in a picture and gave his vital statistics, as he put it when he mentioned it to Herman Busk. Also the local paper, *Lågendalsposten*, gave him a call to arrange an interview, but he asked to be spared so nicely that they realized he really meant it when he said that he didn't want to have a single word in the newspaper, and they left him alone.

He began having stomach pains. After he had eaten. It troubled him and he thought he must see a doctor. But he hoped the pains would go away of themselves, so he put off going to the doctor. They did not. But were the pains really all that intense? He checked how he felt. There was a dull throb of pain, one might say. He had a throb in his teeth and a throb in his stomach. Neither went away. But he did not feel like going to see his good friend Herman Busk, the dentist, in and out of season, choosing to wait until he received his annual reminder. Instead, he decided to go to the doctor. He rang up Dr. Schiøtz at the hospital, to whom he used to go. He knew Dr. Schiøtz in a way, they had both been walk-ons in various musicals staged by the Kongsberg Theater Society, and although that was four years ago, he could still continue to use him as his doctor. Dr. Schiøtz gave him an appointment straightaway.

He showed up at the hospital at the appointed time and was shown into Dr. Schiøtz's office. Seated behind his desk in a white coat, Dr. Schiøtz asked the sort of questions he was used to doctors asking. Bjørn Hansen replied and Dr. Schiøtz nodded. He felt his stomach and asked if it hurt when he pressed. "No, nothing special," Bjørn Hansen said. Dr. Schiøtz wrote out a request for an X-ray as he chatted about the old days, relating en passant that he, too, had given up on the Society. "The years go by," he said. "I prefer to sit at home listening to my Mozart." That, Bjørn Hansen thought, also seemed better suited to this tall, quiet doctor with his long pianist's fingers.

After some time he was given a call by Dr. Schiøtz. He asked him to come to the hospital. The result of the X-ray had come in. Bjørn Hansen turned pale and took himself there at once. He was shown into Dr. Schiøtz's office, where the doctor sat behind his desk like the last time. He was studying the X-ray. "It's impossible to find anything," he said. "We must have more tests. We shall get to the bottom of this." Bjørn Hansen nodded. Dr. Schiøtz listened to Bjørn Hansen's chest with his stethoscope. Quiet, remote, as always. But suddenly he said, "How many patients do you think I've had? In my whole life?" Bjørn Hansen shook his head, astonished at the question. He didn't know what to say. Dr. Schiøtz suddenly looked straight at him, intensely, but with that absent look in his eyes, which everyone had interpreted as reclusiveness and modesty. "To have a completely healthy patient cannot be called satisfying from a physician's point of view, can it? What? It must surely be more satisfying to have someone very ill. It's a sick person, after all, that the physician can cure. Don't you agree?"

Bjørn Hansen felt uneasy. It was so strange here. Dr. Schiøtz had changed, and this was quite unexpected. It was what he said that made the difference, rather than his manner, which was as Bjørn Hansen had always remembered it. Suddenly Bjørn Hansen understood it all. The man was a drug addict, of course. Why hadn't he realized that earlier? Dr. Schiøtz on stage at the Kongsberg Cinema, the two of them, he and Bjørn Hansen, dancing in the chorus and singing the refrain in cowboy outfits or fishermen's jumpers, or whatever it was. Always absent. Never properly "with it," though he was bursting with a restless energy and sang resoundingly, but always with a quiet, idiotic smile on his lips. Oh yes, that was Dr. Schiøtz, the quiet drug addict. Bjørn Hansen felt dizzy. That no one had seen it before! It was so obvious, after all. But it was obvious *now*, and only because Dr. Schiøtz had used this deviant language. In other words, Bjørn Hansen realized it *now* only because Dr. Schiøtz had given him an invitation to realize it.

This made such a violent impression on him that he barely knew what he was doing. He looked incredulously at Dr.

Schiøtz, who sat behind his desk in his white coat, his thin fingers fiddling with the stethoscope and his mild gaze absent. Is this real? Why me? Why does Dr. Schiøtz wish to initiate me of all people in this? But Dr. Schiøtz gave no answer, he just sat there as before, remote and quiet behind his desk. Suddenly Bjørn heard himself say, "What bothers me is that my life is so unimportant." He had never admitted that to a soul before, not even to himself, although it had been on the tip of his tongue for many years, well, all along, and now he said it. He looked in surprise at Dr. Schiøtz. Dr. Schiøtz's absent gaze fluttered, as when someone is moved without wanting to show it. A fluttering, absent gaze, deep inside. "And there are still thirty years to go, or something like that, seventeen in any case until I retire with a pension. I have no illusions, at least I don't think I have." He heard himself talking, aloud and in such a curiously innocent tone of voice. What in the world was this? Dr. Schiøtz's gaze fluttered again. Then he smiled, a heartfelt smile. The contact was made.

His stomach was throbbing. Dr. Schiøtz was busy trying to find out what it was. He inclined toward the view that the stomach pains were a symptom of something else and did several tests. Which were all negative—or positive, depending on what you were looking for. This meant that Bjørn Hansen had several appointments with this most highly respected hospital physician. He could hear himself talking about things that he hadn't even talked about with himself before, while the doctor listened, elated. In a state of mild intoxication, most likely. "Nearly everything is totally indifferent to me," Bjørn Hansen would hear himself say. "Time is passing, boredom is everlasting." Words that made Dr. Schiøtz sincerely glad, he could see, as the doctor was doing his investigations. Could it be the throat? Open your mouth. Could it be the ears? What do the ears have to do with the stomach? Who knows, who knows?

"You know, I find myself in this town by pure chance, it has never meant anything to me. It's also by pure chance that I'm the treasurer here. But if I hadn't been here, I would've been somewhere else and have led the same kind of life. However, I cannot reconcile myself to that. I get really upset when I think about it," Bjørn Hansen said, once more shaken in his innermost self by the fact that he was really expressing himself in this way in the presence of another person. "Existence has never answered my questions," he added. "Just imagine, to live an entire life, my own life at that, without having found the path to where my deepest needs can be seen and heard! I'll die in silence, which frightens me, without a word on my lips, because there's nothing to say," he said, hearing the desperate appeal in his words. Spoken to another person who had long ago ceased to function as a human being, who was nothing but an empty shell in his relations with the society in which he had a high and important position. Oh, that sun shining in through the municipal curtains on the window of this doctor's office at the Kongsberg Hospital! Those nauseating sunbeams in the window frame. The translucent glass in the rectangular windowpanes, sponged down every day as part of the aura of security a hospital must radiate in societies like ours. He was a bit ashamed of his words, for it offended him that a man past fifty spoke about death, and now he had done so himself, loud and clear. A man of thirty can do so, for his death is a disaster, from whatever viewpoint it is seen, being snatched away from his career in one gulp, but for him, Bjørn Hansen, who had recently turned fifty, death would only be the conclusion of a natural process, albeit somewhat early, statistically, and so he simply had to put up with it all, without a whimper, done is done, and the race moves on toward its natural conclusion. Yet he had expressed his horror at having to die without a word to say about it all, not even to himself, and this was, and remained, unbearable to him.

And what did Dr. Schiøtz say to all of this? Not much. He was simply elated. He did his investigations, sealed the tests, sent them for analysis, received the results, summoned Bjørn Hansen to another appointment and did new tests. Meanwhile Bjørn Hansen continued to talk about matters of this kind. It was as if he had entered an altogether different space simply by walking toward Dr. Schiøtz, sitting or standing and with his mild, absent gaze, which occasionally fluttered with a quiet joy that someone had come to him in this way. Now and then he would refer to his drug addiction, always by calling it his "fate." "With my fate," he might say, "it's not so easy to relate to anything at all, even the most quotidian task is a torture to me when I think about it. Oddly enough, not when I do it, but when I think about it, before or after." At long last Dr. Schiøtz had undertaken a complete checkup of Bjørn Hansen's body and had found nothing whatsoever. "There's nothing wrong with you," he said, "that I can guarantee," and then he snickered. It was a bad habit that the doctor had developed in his consultations with Bjørn Hansen. A suppressed snicker, which Bjørn Hansen disliked, but accepted because it meant that Dr. Schiøtz now trusted him so implicitly that he could let out this expression of being caught up in a permanent mild intoxication, which he otherwise had to take great care not to let slip from his innermost being, where he lived his own life, only for himself, in himself, totally indifferent to anything except the intoxication that was wreaking havoc so soothingly in his invisible veins. And with that Bjørn Hansen's role as patient was over. He said thank you and goodbye and left the hospital, a bit surprised that it was over and that these strange sessions were now a closed chapter.

But then Dr. Schiøtz began to seek out Bjørn Hansen privately. In his flat. Mostly late at night, and often more intoxicated than he used to be in his office. He did not come often, maybe once a week, sometimes more seldom. But the conversations continued. Bjørn Hansen talked and Dr. Schiøtz alluded to his fate, which he was glad to be able to give voice to in a natural and straightforward manner. When Dr. Schiøtz had left, Bjørn Hansen continued the conversation by himself, with the doctor as a fictitious interlocutor. In this way he became increasingly absorbed by thinking openly in the language that had somehow taken hold of him. It was all about his inability to reconcile himself to the fact that this was it. He felt outraged. He refused to put up with it. Somehow or other he had to show it, that he refused to put up with it. And so he hatched a plan. An insane project, which he decided to present to Dr. Schiøtz the next time he called.

It was a plan whereby Bjørn Hansen would actualize his No, his great Negation, as he had begun to call it, through an action that would be irrevocable. Through a single act he would plunge into something from which there was no possibility of retreat and which bound him to this one insane idea for the rest of his life. He very much looked forward to presenting it to Dr. Schiøtz, not least because the plan depended on the doctor's cooperation, so that it bound them together in a way that completed the relationship which had by now sprung up between them. He therefore looked forward to Dr. Schiøtz's coming, and when he finally rang the doorbell late one evening, more remote than ever, in another world, one could safely say, Bjørn Hansen heard a peculiarly expectant tone in his own voice when he said, "Ah, it's you, come in, come in!" Dr. Schiøtz sat down and straightaway Bjørn Hansen began to explain his plan, in brief outline. What it consisted of, what Bjørn Hansen was going to do, and why, and where Dr. Schiøtz came into it. However, Dr. Schiøtz said at once that he would not take part in it. It was too risky. But Dr. Schiøtz was completely necessary, without him it could not be implemented. Bjørn Hansen was astonished by the doctor's negative reaction, which suggested that he looked at it as "reality" and not as an "idea," the way it was intended on Bjørn Hansen's part; but if an "idea" is to be carried to its logical conclusion as an "idea," it must be trumpeted as "reality," something that Dr. Schiøtz had not been willing to accept. Maybe the "idea" was no good, Bjørn Hansen thought, trying to explain it further to the doctor. He did not feel he got it quite right. He vouched fully for the "idea," or vision, but had difficulty putting it into words. Not what was going to happen, but why in the world he could take it into his head to think like that, even if only as a game. In the end he simply had to tell him: "I cannot explain why I think as I do," he said. "But that's how I'm thinking, all right," he added, laughing, slightly confused at himself. Shortly afterward Dr. Schiøtz said "Good night" and left.

But he came back. He had changed his mind. "But I want half of the insurance money," he said, something Bjørn Hansen was glad to offer him. "For you're taking a great risk," he said. Dr. Schiøtz gave a shrug.

From then on the doctor tackled the plan. With his expertise, he at once pounced on three weak elements in it. "The place in question cannot be here," he said. "It must be somewhere else altogether. In Eastern Europe, maybe. Do you have any opportunity of going there for a plausible reason?" Bjørn Hansen thought it over. "Yes," he said, "I think so." And then there was one thing that had to be prevented. No one else must get involved. If they could see to that, things would work out. "Those who will come to grips with the problem as part of their everyday routine won't have the least suspicion, that's human nature," the doctor said. "We won't be found out, unless you crack up." But Bjørn Hansen would not crack up. If for nothing else than out of consideration for Dr. Schiøtz. If he should feel an urge to confess, he had someone other than himself to consider, and that would seal his lips, he said passionately, and again he noticed that Dr. Schiøtz was touched.

After the insane "idea" had been gone over in meticulous detail by Dr. Schiøtz, it took on the nature of a clinical operation, in which one dealt with points of surgery, whose alternatives and possible obstacles were carefully reviewed. For now that Dr. Schiøtz had decided to participate actively in the game, he made it very concrete. What from the beginning had been merely an expression of Bjørn Hansen's profound yearning for something irrevocable, now became a feasible project within the structure of the health service, where one had to take advantage of the fact that it is possible to make, from the inside, little holes, thin and dark, in every conceptual system, as well as in every social network.

For Bjørn Hansen, Dr. Schiøtz's espousal of his project meant that it became both more uncanny and more fascinating. Soon he could not tell whether it was a game or real. Well, he was himself of the opinion that it was a game, a sick figment of his imagination—oh yes, that's what he called it, this logic of lunacy in his own brain which he was so fascinated by and which he shared with Dr. Schiøtz, like a vote of confidence. But as one word led to another and he pointed out to Dr. Schiøtz that it was a "game," even insisting on it, though very discreetly, indirectly, Dr. Schiøtz looked scornfully at him, as if he wouldn't budge, failing to understand what Bjørn Hansen meant by referring to a sort of "game." The plan was to be carried out. That was entirely real. They merely lacked a locale, and that would present itself in due course. Dr. Schiøtz was not playing a game. Bjørn Hansen felt a tightening in his throat. Wasn't he the treasurer at Kongsberg? Wasn't Dr. Schiøtz a highly respected doctor at Kongsberg Hospital? What was this anyway? A game that, even as a game, must never reach anyone's ears, the embarrassment would be too great. The treasurer and the doctor. But Dr. Schiøtz was a drug addict. He needed a fellow conspirator, and not only to play a "game." He had taken a personal risk to track down a "healthy" person who spoke the language of the "sick," in earnest, as a fellow conspirator; Dr. Schiøtz did not hesitate to enter into a business agreement with such a brother.

Bjørn Hansen came to feel strongly ambivalent both about Dr. Schiøtz and the plan as the doctor became more and more absorbed in its preparation. He was provoked by the doctor's clinical way of discussing a future event that would leave his life fundamentally altered, indeed, catastrophically altered; it was about a descent into the unknown and the absolutely irrevocable, and since Bjørn Hansen suspected Dr. Schiøtz of eagerly espousing this plan despite the fact that he, as a physician, must consider it to be not only stupid but self-destructive, well, "sick," it must mean that the doctor was trying to make him "fall," because only then could they become equals, beyond everything, each with his own secret suffering. Nevertheless he became so fascinated by the plan, not least its possible execution, that he often thought: "I'll do it. I'll do it, God help me! Nobody can stop me from doing it, at last. But it is insane, of course, insanely tempting, it is madness!" And in the end, when he understood that he was gambling so desperately with his own life that he considered, in all seriousness, to go through with this enterprise, he exclaimed aloud if he was by himself, "No, no, this isn't true! This isn't me!"

But then he had a letter from his son. It arrived at the end of May and took him completely by surprise. He had not seen his son since he was fourteen, when Peter, who lived with his mother and stepfather in Narvik, stopped seeing him in the summer, since it did not fit into the youth's other, more exciting plans. But they had not been completely out of contact. They talked on the telephone several times a year, at Christmas and on birthdays. And Peter had often called him when he had something exceptionally joyful to tell him, as when he had received particularly good marks in school, or his team, or he himself, had excelled on the sports ground. But this was the first time Bjørn had received a letter from him.

Peter Korpi Hansen was now twenty years old. He was in the army and was to be discharged in a few weeks, at the beginning of June. The letter had been posted from his barracks and on the back of the envelope his son had entered his service number before his name, along with the troop and the company to which he belonged. He wrote that come autumn he would start at Kongsberg Engineering College, where he had been admitted to the optics program. In that connection he wondered whether he could stay with his father during the first term, or at least until he had found suitable lodgings at a reasonable price.

Bjørn Hansen was moved. He immediately sat down at his desk and wrote back. Of course Peter could stay with him, nothing would give him more pleasure. He had space enough, so he didn't have to look around for lodgings, unless he preferred to live elsewhere than with his father; if so, he would not be hurt, because he knew that many young men did.

Afterward—because the letter was a bit short, he thought—he added a few lines about his everyday life as town treasurer at Kongsberg. He explained how the hard times had led to an increased workload for him, as people who had lived beyond their means during the good times were unable to meet their obligations when the turnaround came, with the result that the number of bankruptcies had greatly increased, which was regrettable, of course, but something he could do nothing about. *Still, don't imagine it's pleasant for me to put my name to a document that takes away the homes of ordinary people who can no longer meet their obligations*, he wrote. *To tell the truth, it breaks my heart; but my face reveals none of that, because my feelings cannot help those involved anyway.*

After adding a few words to the effect that he looked forward to seeing Peter here at Kongsberg, he signed the letter *Your father*, put it in an envelope and sealed it. He looked about him in the flat. There was space enough for more than one person.

It consisted of four rooms. A large living room, which served as parlor and dining room and had a broad sliding door onto a friendly balcony with evening sunlight. He had a kitchen with all modern facilities, except for a microwave, which was only good for preparing junk food anyway. In addition there were two large bedrooms, one of which Bjørn Hansen had furnished as a library, where he was now writing to his son. To keep the flat clean, he had employed a young girl, who was in her next to last year in secondary school. She was the daughter of Mrs. Johansen at the Treasury and was called Mari Ann. Strictly speaking, he could very well have kept the flat tidy by himself. But Mrs. Johansen had complained that the pressure on young people was so strong today, they must have both this and that, expensive sports equipment as well as brand-name clothing, so that most of them had a part-time job besides going to school, except for her own Mari Ann, which caused her daughter to feel like an outsider, and consequently Bjørn Hansen, Mrs. Johansen's boss, had proposed that her daughter could earn some extra cash cleaning his flat.

And so Mari Ann came and cleaned for him. She was given a set of keys and let herself in whenever it suited her. It didn't matter to him when she came, as long as she came once a week and did the work he paid her to do. Sometimes she was there in the afternoon when he let himself into the flat. She would stand bent over her bucket. It gave off a smell of green soap. She was dressed in tight blue jeans. Entering the living room, he saw her stand there, bent over, wringing out her rag. Absorbed by her work, she presented a round, girlish bottom. She was quite unaffected by his entering the room and observing her. "Hey," she just said, without looking up. Bjørn

Hansen couldn't help smiling (rather sadly?) at this youthful unconcern and naivete, unconcern at any rate about his gaze, which, incidentally, he quickly turned away. At first she was extremely dutiful and thorough, and consequently the job took her a long time. But then she began to rush through her work. One day he had complained about it. He pointed out that the corners, where the dust collects, had not been washed thoroughly enough. Not under the sofa either. Then she blushed. She turned crimson, and the color spread across her cheeks to her very earlobes. It was a strange sight and Bjørn Hansen had become confused. At the same time he was worried that she would tell her mother, and he had no idea how to tackle that. So he said that he had not meant to be nitpicking and difficult, but he really did think a flat wasn't clean unless the whole floor had been washed—so come on, he would help her move the sofa. They moved it together, but the redness did not go away from her earlobes. He did not think, however, that she had said anything at home about it; at any rate, Mrs. Johansen showed no telltale signs in the office.

Bjørn had by this time lived by himself for four years. In this flat. Now he would have to make some changes. First of all, his son would have to be given the library as his room. This meant that the books must be moved into the living room, and he would have to find a place there for reading. Anyway, some of the bookshelves could remain, for Peter's books. Also, he had to buy a bed, or perhaps preferably a sofa bed, turning the room into a kind of sitting room, where his son could receive visitors. No, that could be misunderstood. His son should, of course, receive his visitors in the large living room, for then he could go to *his* bedroom, where he would fit up a reading nook and arrange a little library in miniature, yes, that was how it must be done. Though his son ought to have a sofa bed all the same—after all, he could receive his friends in the living room even if he had a sofa bed, hell yes, a bed would make it feel too bedroomish. And then he had to consider buying a microwave in spite of everything. True, he maintained that you couldn't possibly prepare really good food in a microwave, but for a busy young student who was likely to want a bite of something in a hurry, it was probably an excellent arrangement, he thought.

And so he wandered about in the flat, planning the changes that were forced upon him because his son was coming to stay. He was excited. This would turn his whole existence upside down. He actually had a son who was coming to live with him. It was an undeserved joy and he understood that he ought to appreciate it. He tore down the bookshelves in his cherished library, except for one which he thought would suit Peter's books to perfection. Started rigging them up in the living room. He also made a reading nook in his own bedroom, with a bookcase along one wall and a good easy chair to sit in. The son's room was now completely crammed with books, in piles on the floor. Before putting them in place, in the living room and in his own bedroom, he took a stroll about town to look for a good sofa bed. And a microwave. When he returned he put the books on the shelves. In a few days the sofa bed arrived. Bjørn Hansen walked about in the flat, wondering if he had forgotten anything, something that a young student must have in his bedroom, which might also become his study. "Finally something to look forward to!" he exclaimed. "Yes, I must say! This I hadn't expected. To think that he is going to live here, if only for a few weeks! How wonderful that he intends to become an optician! And also that he was admitted! My whole existence will be turned upside down!"

He was going to be reunited with his son. It was Peter who had not stayed in touch. But he was also the one who now took the initiative to restore contact. Bjørn knew it could be difficult. Six years had passed since he last saw Peter and then his son was a child, now he was an adult. He didn't even know what he looked like. Perhaps he had not wanted to break contact with his father when he was fourteen. Though he had found an excuse not to visit every summer. Maybe he had hoped that his father would beg him to come on bended knee. That, however, Bjørn had not done, because losing contact was part of the price he had paid for abandoning his little son of two, and his mother. That's why he simply put up with hearing this son, on turning fourteen, telling his father that he had altogether different plans for the summer than visiting him, and that this is repeated when the son turns fifteen, sixteen, seventeen, eighteen ... As the time of Peter's arrival approached, Bjørn realized more and more clearly how uncertain and scared he felt about this meeting. He observed it in the way he talked to others about his son's coming. To Berit and Herman Busk, for example. He spoke about Peter like an altogether ordinary father. He would remark, casually, that it would not be easy having a young man in the house, and he expressed a paternal concern as to whether the study of optics was "good enough." It was as if he were practicing to take on a role he had not even considered for eighteen years, and which he now tried to make everyone believe was made for him. But he gave himself away to the eighteen-year-old Mari Ann, who cleaned his flat. Because of the changes he had made in the flat, he told her he expected his son in the autumn. Then she suddenly became interested and asked, quite naturally in fact, if he had a photo of him. But he didn't! The most recent photograph he had of his son showed Peter on a summer's day the year he turned eleven. Mari Ann stared, openmouthed. Afterward Bjørn Hansen could see to his annoyance that she had tried to hide what she really thought about a fifty-year-old man who seemed to care so little about his son. The girl clearly felt fully justified in her moral condemnation, which was not lessened by her attempt to act as if nothing were the matter, having initially gaped in wonder, because she did not dare to show openly what she thought of him. After all, he was the one who gave her pocket money and, moreover, he was old and a sort of pillar of society. And he was her mother's boss.

Actually, he had felt no need for having photos of Peter as he grew up. If he had got some, it would have been nice, but not having any did not make him feel deprived. He did not feel a tremendous urge to know how his son looked on his eighteenth birthday, the day he received his matriculation certificate, or the day he left for his military service. He had a son, that was enough for him, and he felt little need to speculate on how he looked. He saw no reason for having a familial relationship with his son, because they did not belong to the same family, nor had they ever done so except for a brief spell. But Peter was his son. He was proud to have a son, but under the circumstances he felt no need for that son to have a face that he might contemplate in a photograph. And he wouldn't have an eighteen-year-old girl staring at him as if he were some kind of monster because of it.

He had often thought about his son over the years. Not

night and day. Nor had he ever lain awake wondering how he was getting on. He had assumed that Peter would lead his own life, without him, growing from a child to a man without having him nearby, as a corrective. He liked the thought of his son running about in Narvik and growing up. When Peter still visited in the summertime, he looked forward to it, and he spent a fortnight with him, which was rich in high points; but when the fortnight came to an end, it was only with sadness, rather than sorrow, that he drove him to Fornebu and took him to the plane that was to take him back to his home in Narvik. Indeed, to tell the truth, he felt a kind of relief that it was over, that it had gone well, and that he could now resume his customary life. Still, it was these fourteen summer days each year, from the time when Peter was a little boy, that connected him directly to his son. He knew very well that Peter was now a young man, far removed from the little Peter of his boyhood days, and it was likely to make the young man embarrassed if reminded of them. It was not Peter but memories that Bjørn Hansen had preserved, all but palpably. Such as twitches in the small boy's hand at the sight of a big stray dog right in front of them, which he feels because he is holding Peter's hand. The boy who stops short, clutching his father's hand to hold him back. The boy's fear before a big stray dog, combined with his realization that he must learn to control this or at least not betray it, acting like his father, who says there is no danger, come on! Bjørn felt glad that this tug on his hand was intact inside him. Yes, Bjørn Hansen thought, luckily it was. But how would that help when he met the young stranger who was on his way to Kongsberg to study optics and who was to live, at least for the time being, with him? This twenty-year-old with a face he had never seen before? Who would suddenly appear. Here. To live with his father.

And so, there he stands one morning at the end of August. At Kongsberg Railway Station. Waiting for the train. Waiting for his unknown son. Being early, he was waiting on the platform. Suddenly he caught sight of Dr. Schiøtz, who was also waiting for the train. For some preparations for the hospital. Bjørn Hansen found it rather strange that Dr. Schiøtz picked up the preparations himself, but assumed that he did so because he wanted some fresh air. Bjørn Hansen told him that he was waiting for his son, who was about to begin studying optics at Kongsberg Engineering College. "Your son? I didn't know you had a son. How nice," said the doctor, making Bjørn Hansen wonder whether there was a trace of irony in his voice. But there was no time to think about that, because now the train from Oslo could be seen on the attractively curved railway track. The long train glided slowly into the station and stopped. It was the South Country Express, which halted briefly at Kongsberg before going farther inland, down through Telemark, before it finally reached the coast at the southernmost point of Norway, Kristiansand. Bjørn Hansen craned his neck, for now the passengers were getting off and making their way among those who were waiting to get on.

Bjørn Hansen was struck by the fact that most of those who got off the South Country Express today were young people, especially young men. All with luggage. It was obviously because a new academic year was at hand, and the students were now arriving at Kongsberg after a well-earned holiday, or for the first time. But for Bjørn Hansen this was an unforeseen obstacle, because how could he locate his son among this multitude of young men, all of whom were students! As he watched them coming down the platform toward him, he suddenly felt an intense fear that he would greet the wrong one by mistake. Pick out the wrong son. In the presence of Dr. Schiøtz. It would have laid him low, as the saying goes, as if lightning were suddenly to strike from a clear sky and hit him, on purpose. "There he is," he heard Dr. Schiøtz say. "Your spitting image."

It was Peter. In the row of young men who were just now coming toward him and Dr. Schiøtz he was the only one who moved with a purpose, lugging two heavy suitcases as he steered straight at Bjørn. Of course! Peter recognized him, he hadn't changed that much over the years. He noticed his son's purposeful steps and his eyes fixed on him, then walked forward to put some distance between himself and Dr. Schiøtz when he welcomed his son. As he took these steps, Peter stopped, put down his luggage and smiled. Bjørn Hansen gave a start. It was a younger version of himself. What a naked face, he thought. My own flesh and blood. Such a naked face! It's almost obscene.

By now Bjørn Hansen had reached him. They were facing each other. He resolutely held out his hand. He wanted to shake his son's hand. This because he was afraid that Peter had put down his suitcases so that he would to have his arms free to embrace his father, something that Bjørn Hansen wished to avoid. His son had popped up so suddenly! It would be too intimate to embrace. So he held out his hand. Peter shook it. "Welcome!" the father said. "Hello!" said the son, smiling.

They looked at one another. Apart from the fact that he was a younger version of himself, Peter Korpi Hansen did in no way stand out from the other students who had got off the train here in Kongsberg; indeed, had he not directed his steps so purposefully toward Bjørn Hansen and instead hurried past like the others, Bjørn Hansen might not have singled him out as the son he was there to meet. He was dressed in a T-shirt under a light jacket of some thin synthetic material, which gave him a slightly casual and carefree air. The T-shirt had some letters printed on it, which was probably the case with all T-shirts nowadays. Peter's shirt read, VOICE OF EUROPE. Oddly enough, Bjørn Hansen knew that this was the brand name of a new Norwegian textile manufacturer of fashionable garments for young people, and he knew this because, as treasurer, he was often the State or municipal representative on estate boards, after bankruptcies; in Kongsberg, too, there had been a number of bankruptcies among fashionable shops during the last year, so he knew Voice of Europe, because the firm had filed its claims with the bankrupt party in Kongsberg, and Bjørn Hansen's task was to see to it that the State secured its rightful due, nearly always concerning nonpayment of VAT, which had to be collected before the private creditors took their cut; thus viewed, he was actually a competitor of the firm that his son so naively advertised on his chest, something Peter, naturally, couldn't know, he thought with a small inward smile. He observed his modern young son, who for the rest was dressed in gray summer slacks of a soft, slightly downy stuff, which gave every impression of being pleasant to wear, as even such an untrained eye as Bjørn Hansen had in this branch of business could see. Peter's feet sported heavy, complacent track shoes.

The young man made a tremendous impression on Bjørn Hansen. Because he was his son. Peter's youthfulness struck him so strongly he could scarcely breathe. Youth and all its glories! Prizes to be plucked, a life to be lived, all of this so self-importantly represented in his own son's getup. Bjørn Hansen knew, of course, that his son came across as something of a stereotype. All young men dressed like this nowadays. Youths like Peter Korpi Hansen were ten a penny. All of them radiated the same intoxicating nonchalance, self-indulgence and idleness. Nevertheless it was strange to encounter it in his own son. He had a son who belonged to the youth culture. That son, in all his youthfulness, had adapted to the demands of his own generation. The young man at once began to tell him about his long journey. He had been traveling for more than forty-eight hours by bus and train. Straight through most of Norway. Recumbent in a reclining chair at night, feeling the characteristic nocturnal rhythm of the train. Passing through changing landscapes during the day. Mountains and hillsides. Lakes and small villages. But none of this occupied him now. Traveling was obviously no great experience. He spoke in a loud voice, in a rather preachy manner, his father thought. Peter informed him that he had been the object of an insult. He did not say "insult," but used another, more youthful word. They had tried to dump on him, it must have been. It had happened on the last lap of his journey, from Oslo to Kongsberg. Someone had taken his seat. His reserved seat. His father bent over the suitcases and said, "Well, let's go then." He took them both and Peter did not protest. That seemed, in and of itself, to be a bit strange, but he took it to mean that his son thought he would only be carrying the suitcases to his car, just in front of the station. But when he said, "I didn't take the car, because it's right nearby," his son made no move to relieve him of one of the suitcases, leaving him to carry them both—they were not as heavy as he had imagined, by the way—while Peter went on and on about the insult he had suffered. Well, yeah, when he boarded the train in Oslo, at the carriage indicated, and went to the assigned seat, a lady was sitting there. To be on the safe side, he checked his ticket again before speaking up, informing her that this seat was taken. But the lady said it was not. He showed her his ticket, but she held her own. The train started moving and Peter just stood there, without a seat. The lady refused to budge; she said the reserved seats were marked on the back. There was no such mark on the back of this seat, consequently the seat was not reserved, and so she was entitled to sit there, because she got there first. Peter decided not to temper justice with mercy. He stood bolt upright before the lady occupying his seat, waiting for the conductor. Eventually, when the train was entering Drammen Station, the conductor arrived. Peter handed him the ticket and pointed at his reservation. The conductor looked at it and said, sure, that was correct. But why couldn't he take another seat, since there were several empty ones? Peter had looked at the conductor in amazement. Did he hear correctly? Yes, he heard correctly. All he had to do was take another seat. After all, there were plenty of vacant seats. "But this is my seat. This is the one I've paid for!" The conductor looked at him, annoyed. "Listen, this is nothing to make a fuss about. Sit down, or you can remain standing. You'll be there in just half an hour. Do what you like." And with that he had left. The lady who had taken Peter's seat tossed her head. But Peter had remained standing. All the way to Kongsberg. Without sitting down. Right next to his seat. The conductor had come through that long, narrow carriage once again and

Peter had just stood there. The conductor had hurried past without saying a word. The lady had smiled at the conductor, and Peter had seen the conductor return her smile. But he had remained standing.

Yes, he had remained standing. Bolt upright. In his casual youthful getup, loose and self-indulgent, and with my facial features, Bjørn Hansen thought. The insult. While his father lugged the two heavy suitcases, Peter kept talking about this insult without a break on their way to the block of flats where Bjørn Hansen lived, as his father let himself in at the entrance door and they passed the letterbox, where his father picked up the mail in passing, went over to the lift, where he pressed the button and they waited for the lift to come, entered the lift, which carried them three stories up, where they stepped out onto the landing, the son talking until the very moment when Bjørn Hansen unlocked the flat and they entered the hall, where his father put down the two suitcases.

Bjørn Hansen showed Peter the flat. First, the large living room with the balcony facing west, to which he opened the door. Then the kitchen, before barely opening the door to his own bedroom. He let his son inspect the bathroom, then finally opened the door wide to the room he had furnished for Peter. The son had all along nodded approval of what he saw, and this applied also to the last room, with its sofa bed, bookcase, writing desk and chair, chest of drawers and cabinet, as well as an armchair. He said he could well imagine living here. All autumn. Yes, it would feel good not having to walk about trying to find a furnished room. Nice to have one here. But.

"What is your price?" "Price?"

"Yes, per month."

The father: "Nothing."

The son: "Then it's a deal. This suits me fine. We are living in a tough world."

That last remark was made in his usual high-pitched voice, apropos of nothing in particular, and in the preachy manner that Bjørn Hansen had understood was his son's way of expressing himself. But in this last remark something else had been added: a secretiveness. It was not preachiness in the sense of telling you something for your own good, it was a statement to his father about something he could vouch for, and about which Bjørn Hansen could not have a clue. When he said, "We are living in a tough world," Bjørn Hansen should not by any means assume that Peter could just as well have said, "We are living in a tough world, you know." No, these two assertions were like fire and water; moreover, the way the son conveyed his code contained a peculiar kind of pent-up pride.

Peter said he would unpack at once and went into the hall to get the luggage. He placed the suitcases on the sofa bed one after the other before unpacking. In spite of the fact that there were two large cases, Bjørn Hansen noticed with increasing amazement, as his son unpacked and put the things neatly in place, that he had brought almost nothing with him. That is to say, very few personal items. In one suitcase he had practically nothing except bed linen. A good quality giant eiderdown took up most of the space. The other suitcase contained mostly clothes. The son sorted them and put them nicely away in the wardrobe and the chest of drawers. Underwear, thin socks, thick socks, handkerchiefs, ties, gloves and mittens in separate drawers. Shirts, colored and white, in separate drawers in the left section of the wardrobe, T-shirts in a third and sweaters in a fourth drawer of the wardrobe's left section; trousers and sportswear on hangers in the wardrobe's right section. He asked permission to hang his outdoor things in the hall wardrobe and did so at once, at the same time putting his shoes there, including two pairs of running shoes besides the pair he was wearing, which he found a place for at the bottom of the right-hand section of the wardrobe. He also had an enormously large toilet bag, which he asked to be allowed to keep in the bathroom. There was barely space for it on the bathroom shelf, which was too narrow for the modern age.

Of personal items there were only three, as far as Bjørn Hansen could make out, which the son handled with great affection, but which utterly astonished his father. First, Peter took out a souvenir from his home town, Narvik. It was an inexpensive thing with a base of imitation silver, on which stood a thin pole of the same imitation silver, and on that pole hung the flag of the city of Narvik. Peter spent a lot of time finding just the right place for this article, but after much toing and froing he decided to give it pride of place on the bookcase. Then he took a beer glass out of the suitcase, from among the clothes (Peter had unpacked these two items before unpacking and arranging his clothes, but after unpacking the suitcase with the eiderdown and the rest of the bed linen). This beer glass had a special shape, being an accurate replica, in glass, of a boot. "A two-liter," the son explained, and his father understood that, since he had transported this beer glass (which he noticed had an inscription stating that it belonged to a restaurant in the village where his son had done his military service) by bus and train through most of Norway, it must be associated with a personal experience. Although Peter did not reveal what this was, Bjørn Hansen assumed that it must be one of two things. Either Peter had smuggled it away with him, to the great jubilation of his military chums, after a lively evening at the local pub. Or Peter had impressed them all by tossing off this two-liter glass filled with beer in one draught, without stopping, or he had done so in less time than the others and thereby won the beer boot as a trophy, whether given it by the pub or by his military friends, who had made off with it. Bjørn Hansen did not like to quiz him directly, but tried to worm it out of him by hypocritically showing a great interest in it. This flattered Peter, he could see, but only with the result that his son seemed even more determined to hold on to the mystery of how this two-liter beer boot came to be found in the possession of Peter Korpi Hansen. Therefore he had a tremendously stuck-up air as he tried to find the most suitable place for it. After some more toing and froing, it ended up next to the town flag of Narvik on the top shelf.

Finally, when the two suitcases were empty, Peter revealed the third and last personal item that was to adorn his room in his new life as a student at Kongsberg Engineering College. He took out a tube and rolled out a poster. He hung it on the wall above the sofa bed. After putting it up—by means of drawing pins that Bjørn Hansen had hurriedly produced from a kitchen drawer—Peter took a couple of steps back and admired the poster. Yes, he really admired it. Bjørn Hansen, too, had to come and see it.

It was an enormous poster of a red sports car. Of Italian design. Ferrari. Beside the car, leaning against the door and with his hand self-confidently caressing the chassis, a man in sunglasses. The owner. Sportily dressed. The car was photographed completely open, that is, with the hood rolled back. The background, which was somewhat diffuse, almost desertlike, sandy, emphasized the car's color, which was very fine. The image was purely commercial, displaying the car's dimensions and its gorgeous appearance. There was no trace of irony in the expression of the man next to it, a rarity in modern advertising, just as the image as a whole was totally devoid of irony. It emphasized the expensiveness of the car and, consequently, the power of the man who could lean against it. Nothing else. The absence of irony highlighted the fact that one now found oneself in an atmosphere in which there was no need to put on airs, or apologize with a charming grimace. The raw beauty of wealth. It was gorgeous, and banal. It left only one question: Why had his son brought this poster along and now hung it up on his wall?

The father, however, did not ask any questions about it. And Peter gave no explanation, probably because he thought it spoke for itself. Instead he looked at his watch. He had meant to visit the Engineering College, to survey the situation, as he said. Would look round a bit, drop by the office of the optometry program in any case, to inform them that he had arrived and accepted the course he had applied for and been assigned to. His father asked whether they should not perhaps have dinner together today, here, in the flat, since it was his first day, but Peter could not. He had too much to do, he said, so he did not know when he would be back. The son left and, shortly afterward, Bjørn Hansen left too. For the office. He came back at the usual time. Prepared dinner, ate it, put the dirty dishes in the dishwasher and settled down with a book. Naturally he felt in a peculiar state of mind, restless, preoccupied and without a clue as to how he should handle this new turn of events in his life.

The son returned much earlier than Bjørn Hansen expected. It was not even half past seven when he let himself in. His father was sitting in the living room reading a book, *The Concept of Dread* by Søren Kierkegaard, and once again he could not help marveling at the mind of this nineteenth-century Dane, who, by dealing with biblical myths in real earnest—as if, say, Adam and Eve had really lived, which, indeed, Søren Kierkegaard believed, that Bjørn Hansen had not the least reason to doubt—was able to breathe new life into some fundamental dogmatic concepts as old as the hills that had long been stone-dead for Bjørn Hansen. He perceived a presence and an intensity steam up from the book's pages, taking hold of the mind of this godless tax collector in a Norwegian provincial town toward the end of the twentieth century. One hundred and fifty years of historical darkness and impenetrability had been pierced by a light, which reached this tax collector at Kongsberg—how strange! Though perhaps it was not to be wondered at, for, from a historical perspective, he had come down in the world, his profession having undergone a transformation, downgraded from government official to civil servant, the effect of which was that he could now think of the outsider and mocker of government officials Søren Kierkegaard as a secret ally, although in his daily life he had, of course, no sense of how his livelihood had deteriorated in the course of time, but it no doubt made him extra sensitive to the musicality of Søren Kierkegaard's delving into such dogmatic and (to him) deadly true concepts. The edition he had was published in 1962, so he had first read the book when he was a young student. It was full of underlinings, which he now and then could not help smiling at, now and then being surprised by—gosh, had he really thought this sentence was so important that he had to underline it at the age of twenty-one, the same age Peter was now and with the same naked face—especially as he had read this book in his free time, con amore, not as part of his course, which was in economics, after all, where one was working with entirely different concepts and methods. But there was the click in the door and Peter coming home, just before the *Daily News Roundup*. Bjørn Hansen got up and turned on the TV. The son came into the living room and they sat together watching the *Daily News Roundup*. It was as though they were a sort of family, because that was how they sat, gathered around the daily news on TV, like thousands and thousands of families all over Norway. Bjørn Hansen and his adult son, whom he barely knew but who now sat there in his modern getup, eager to enter upon the race of life, to take the first steps on the road that would bind him to an occupation, which he would stay in and live on for the rest of his life—this son of his, that is, who had taken the first steps on the road that was to turn him into a man, probably a paterfamilias when the time came, someone who for eight hours a day would sit bent over instruments designed to correct a weakened eye so that it could function like a normal one; a man, probably a paterfamilias, in a white smock bent over optical instruments and ground glass precisely adjusted to the concept of the perfect eye. Strange to sit like this, in a family idyll, with an almost totally unknown young stranger, but one he knew was his own son.

Peter, however, seemed little affected by the solemn partaking of this traditional daily family ritual with his father for the first time. He had returned to the flat with a bagful of books, papers, notebooks and binders, and had immediately gone to his room. He had then come back, sat down on the sofa to watch the *Daily News Roundup* for a moment, gone back to his room, come out again, sat down on the sofa and watched the *Daily News Roundup* to the end. He appeared excited, but also slightly restless.

When the *Daily News Roundup* was over, his father asked if he could turn off the TV. Peter nodded, it was OK with him. They sat in silence for a while, until the son suddenly said, "Algot hasn't come." Bjørn Hansen asked who Algot was and received the reply that Algot was Peter's friend and at the same time his good genius. He said the latter in a straightforward tone, causing his father to be taken aback, for he had never heard anyone describe a friend as his good genius before. Despite having made up his mind not to appear intrusive with his son, continually bombarding him with questions, he could not resist the temptation to do exactly that to find out as much as possible about Algot and his relationship to Peter.

Peter had met Algot in the military. They had been in the same platoon and lived in the same room throughout the service. They had become good friends. And it was Algot who had made Peter apply for admission to the optometry program at the Kongsberg Engineering College. Before that, the idea would never have occurred to Peter, who barely knew what optics was. He had no idea what he would take up, but had considered a number of professions. He had considered computer science, media studies too, as possibilities. Actually, he had started a correspondence course in computer science; there were many good offers of correspondence courses in the military, and he had enrolled in computer science, like so many others. But Algot had said, "Computer science? There will be a surplus of people going in for computer science. In a few years, I think, we'll see long queues of dissatisfied computer consultants, computer engineers and computer programmers in their early thirties in front of the retraining desk at the job centers. So forget it!" Algot was going to study optics. That was not particularly surprising, for Algot was called Blom, and Algot Blom was the name of an optical firm in Oslo which had several shops in the capital and also planned to establish itself in other Norwegian cities. Naturally, Algot Blom was going to study optics, he was the heir to a veritable empire in that field. But he made Peter want to study optics too. The way he spoke about the profession made Peter interested in it. Because it had a great future ahead of it. It was not a profession only for someone whose father had an optician's shop in his home town, far from it; in the coming years there would be an enormous need for people who had optics as their engineering speciality. That was the expression Algot had used. Optics as a speciality within the field of engineering. Anyway, he made Peter take a couple of correspondence courses which could be seen as an introduction to the study of optics. Dealing with optics in general. This was at the beginning of their military service. Algot had taken the same course, so they studied together, just the two of them, and since Algot already knew a lot about the subject it went like clockwork. And when Algot last spring had applied to be admitted to the optometry program at Kongsberg Engineering College, starting in the autumn, Peter had done the same. It now seemed perfectly natural to him to seek admission to a field of study which, a few months ago, had not even entered his thoughts, with a view to making it his livelihood, for life. One might well remark upon the role played by chance in all this, but optics was a clever choice. That would soon become evident. Someone who chooses to obtain a degree in a small field with great future potential, but not altogether "in," is wiser than someone who pounces on a subject of study that everyone is talking about, because it is always those who first see the potential of a subject and are bold enough to gamble on it who will enjoy the fruits of it once it has become "in," and Peter had not the least doubt that optics would be "in." Without being told straight out, his father understood that Peter had taken into consideration his friendship with Algot Blom when he chose his field of study. Not only had he selected a subject long before it would be extremely popular, but also he would, as a fully trained optician with a stream of new opticians behind him, benefit from his friendship with Algot. For there were more Algot Blom shops than Algot himself could manage. Therefore Peter often entertained the thought that, in a few years, he would manage a large optician's shop in Oslo or be sent out to take over an optician's in, for example, Kristiansand or Stavanger in Algot Blom's name. It did not bother him in the least that this meant Algot would be his boss, because Algot was his friend. They had stuck together through thick and thin during their military service. Both inside the camp and in the town, on leave. What the two of them had experienced in town together could fill a whole novel, the son said, laughing. In particular, all those stories about how they had sneaked in without being seen, having stayed out beyond the time at which they were to report back to camp, would make people crack up with laughter if they were written down by a real author. Both had felt almost sad when they were discharged. But they were going to study together in the autumn, after all. He had heard from Algot in the summer. Then they had agreed to meet at Kongsberg today. They had not decided on a definite place or time; the town was not large, so they were bound to bump into each other, as Algot had said. But Peter had not found him. Not in the Engineering College. Not in the street. Not in any of the many pubs and restaurants where he had dropped in. He had the impression that the town was full of students, at least a thousand, who had inundated the streets and the pubs. But no Algot. He had been looking for him all day. Even at the Central Station in Oslo this morning, in case Algot had also taken the train, though he found this hard to believe as Algot was sure to have his own car. It was rather odd. After all, college would start tomorrow. "He will come at the very last moment, then," his father said. "There are many like that."—"But we had an agreement," Peter said, feeling wronged.—"Maybe he changed his mind," his father said. "Perhaps he thought he could benefit from a year of practice in one of the family businesses. Have you thought about that?"—"But his name is on the list," Peter said obstinately. "I asked if he was there and they looked for his name and said that, yes, he's there. So he'll be coming."

Bjørn Hansen had a son in the house. The son had come and had put up at his place. He had unpacked his things. He had been out to inspect the college that was to be his admission ticket to adulthood with all its imperatives and obligations, which are the very bedrock upon which we construct the reality we like to call life. On the threshold of life. His first day. And then his good genius, Algot, hadn't shown up. In spite of the fact that they had an agreement. When a twenty-year-old tells his father that we live in a tough world, what does it mean?

When he also glorifies a poster advertising a red sports car as if it were high art? It was evening in Kongsberg. Evening in the treasurer's living room. An evening in August. Dark and mild. The door to the balcony was ajar, so that the cool breeze could be felt in the room, but just barely. So, Peter has decided to study optics because he has a friend who will do so, the father thought. Otherwise he would never have done it. Well, life is full of fortuitous circumstances, of course, and our choices, not least where study is concerned, may depend on the oddest things. But it is the friend who has chosen for him. That's it. It doesn't have to mean an awful lot, but I'm worried about him, Bjørn Hansen thought. Especially since—but here his thoughts stopped short, because he happened to think of his son's much too loud voice, which had irritated and troubled him all along, and that he found both profoundly unjust and frightening.

Peter had stepped out on the balcony. He was getting a breath of fresh air. Bjørn Hansen followed and stood beside his son. A soft August evening, dark. Dark sky. Dark air. Dark because of the steep hills that surrounded Kongsberg. In between the hills, the town was illuminated by a scattering of dim lights. Down here, out there. Dim lights from the shop windows and the streetlamps. From the service station below them, slightly to the left, with its enormous lifeless sheet of asphalt, came a dim light, likewise from a lone window in the Gyldenløve Hotel, the fourth floor. The platform of the railway station, with no trains, was dimly lit, and a dim light from a streetlamp hovered over a lone taxi parked by the stand outside the station. Barely a sound came from the town itself, straight ahead of them and below. But a steady hum could still be heard. It came from far away, at the outer edge of the area visible from the balcony, on both sides. On the left were the cars on the main road to Oslo, on the right the cars on the way to Geilo and Bergen. These two main roads went in a circle around Kongsberg, along with a third main road, the road to Notodden and over Haukelifjell to the West Country, but that one did not come within sight or sound of the two men standing on the balcony. But the two main roads that did, if only for a short distance, were brightly illuminated, much more so than the city streets, whose dim, scattered illumination was intensified by the strong floodlights shining above the roadway along which the cars, with their small moving yellow lights and their steady hum, were driving. From the town directly opposite and below them, in the middle of which they actually found themselves, came scarcely a sound. Now and then a car door being slammed, followed by an engine being turned on and revved up. A sudden laugh, interrupted. A car driving slowly along the street, two blocks off, and a streak of light just before it reaches the corner, which they can see from their vantage point on the balcony. Then footsteps on the asphalt directly below. And Lågen, the small bend of it to their right, just before the brightly illuminated main road to Geilo and Bergen, was completely still, a mere dark hole as seen from the balcony. "Look!" Peter said and pointed. He pointed at a neon sign on the other side of the railway station, the sign which said that this was where CITY, the supermarket, was located. But it was not the supermarket that interested Peter, but the sign. That red neon sign. CITY. "We're in CITY," he said, enraptured, but still with a residue of preachiness in his voice. In the middle of CITY. "Look!" he said again, pointing. This time at another bright sign, also in red neon. It hung at the top of a tall mast, almost at the level of the balcony they were standing on. TOYOTA, it shined. "Fantastic!" Peter said. "This is powerful. I feel I'll be happy here, my blood is fired up," he declared. "And tomorrow Algot will come."

He abruptly tore himself away from the sight of Kongsberg by night and went back to the living room. The father thought his son had been inspired to plunge into the disco world, which in Kongsberg, too, thrived in basements where violent, pounding music and superfast flashing lights produced a youthful enthusiasm, but, being played in basements, behind strictly guarded doors, such as, among other places, deep underground at the Grand Hotel, that music had not betrayed itself to the two standing on a third-floor balcony in this modern block of flats in the middle of Kongsberg, but it existed, and Bjørn Hansen thought that it had now enticed Peter. But no. His son wanted to go to bed. He had to get up early tomorrow. He liked to get a good night's sleep. The city and its loud rhythms would have to wait. Until he and Algot would go there together. The son went to the bathroom, to get ready for the night. Or as his father thought, "To make his toilet for the night," for he could not help noticing the huge toilet bag that Peter had brought with him. What did he have in that damn bag? He decided, however, that regardless of how intrigued he might be by his son's doings, he would never look into this bag, because he had convinced himself that it contained secrets he was reluctant to be initiated into. But his son certainly did not try to keep it secret. He could have kept the bag in his room, but instead he placed it on the glass shelf in the bathroom. And there it still was when at long last he came out of the bathroom.

Wearing a bathrobe, he quietly ambled to his room and closed the door behind him, after first saying a brief goodnight. A gentleman, Bjørn Hansen thought, my son is a modern young gentleman. Well, well. He's here now in any case. As a guest in my existence, he thought.

Algot did not come. Bjørn Hansen saw his young son go to his first day of instruction excited, a bit nervous, with newly purchased books in a bag, ballpoints, paper for notetaking, ring binders. On the threshold of life, ready to absorb knowledge. In a new T-shirt inscribed BIK BOK. But when he returned in the evening he was down in the dumps, though he tried to hide it. That Bjørn Hansen could see. His son let himself in and was heading at full speed for his room when he stopped, duty bound, to exchange a few words with his father, who knew that it had been his first day at college. "We are forty," he said. "In the class. Carefully filtered out," he added. "From all over the Nordic countries, even one from Iceland. One staff member is a professor from England. He doesn't live here but flies over once a week to teach us. NIT in Trondheim will send an expert from its Lighting Engineering Lab as soon as the need arises. I must say the setup is professional." He was talking apropos of nothing, over the head of his father and with his face partly turned away. Then he said he had to study and hurried to his room, where he spent several hours. Late in the evening he came out in his dressing gown and went to the bathroom. He stayed a long time in there, then shuffled quietly out and went to his room. "Algot didn't come," he said as he opened the door. "But he'll probably turn up tomorrow," he added.

He didn't. Peter came home in the early afternoon, when his

father was having dinner; he asked if Peter would like to share his meal with him, but he shook his head. He was not hungry. On the other hand, he was indignant. "Algot won't be coming," he said. "And the college doesn't give a damn. They're simply leaving his place open. Because they haven't had any message from him."

"But then he's likely to come, don't you think?" Bjørn Hansen said, "he's just been delayed for a few days."—"No," Peter said, "for Algot is in London, I've found out."

The last words were uttered with a gloating expression on his face, which Bjørn Hansen did not think suited his son. For Peter had put things straight. What the college had not managed, young Korpi Hansen had undertaken to clear up. When Peter had entered the classroom for the first period, he had taken his stand and surveyed the scene. He was expecting to catch sight of Algot, who then would have winked at him or revealed himself in some other way: "Well, here I am, on the second day of instruction! That's not half bad, eh?" But Algot was not there. Peter looked around the room, silently counting everyone present, himself included. Thirty-nine. There should have been forty. Then he sat down and followed the first period, in physiology, though he had found it hard to concentrate. As soon as the break came, he had run up to the office. They recognized him from yesterday. He again asked if it was really true that they had not heard from Algot Blom. They replied, with a resigned air, that they had not. "But he hasn't come!" Peter erupted.—"Well, no, but we haven't received any message."—"Is that quite certain?" Peter asked. "Couldn't you check once more?" he said. But the office girl refused. Then Peter became indignant, but fortunately he controlled himself.

He simply turned sharply about and swept out. Not to go to his next class, which had already begun, by the way, but to the Wire Service Office. There he had opened the Oslo telephone book at *B* and searched the pages (with furious, agitated fingers, his father thought) until he found Algot Blom's private address, which Peter had assumed must be that of his parents. He had entered a phone booth and punched in the number. No answer. Next he had looked up the number of the main store of the Algot Blom firm, had entered the booth, had once again called the number. He had asked to speak to the manager. The manager, however, was occupied just then, and the voice on the line, a man's, asked what it was about. "It concerns Algot Blom, Jr," Peter said. "I'm a close friend of his. Do you know how I can get in touch with him? I mean, do you know where he is just now?"—"Junior?" the voice said. "Junior went to London the day before yesterday."

"And when will he be back?"—"For Christmas," the voice replied. "As far as I know. When they get their Christmas holiday."—"Ah, yes," Peter said. "So he chose to study optometry in London, after all."—"Precisely," said the voice. "Only the best is good enough, you know." Peter put down the receiver.

Afterward he regretted having hung up so quickly. He could have asked for Algot's address and telephone number. But he had become so confused. However, since he had passed himself off as Algot's friend, which he was of course, he could not let it appear he had no idea that he had gone to London to study optometry. He had said nothing to Peter about that. "We'll meet at Kongsberg in the autumn," he had said. But instead he had opted for the more famous optometry course at City University in London. Peter had at once gone back to the office. He did not say that Algot was in London, but only asked them again whether they would consider checking if Algot Blom, Jr, had left a message that would explain the fact that he had failed to show up, now that instruction in the optometry program had begun. But the office girl would not. Nor would her superior, a man who turned up just as Peter was repeating his question. Well, he insisted that they check into it. They might have overlooked something. Had Algot written and renounced his place, perhaps? If so, there was a vacancy. Didn't they understand? That if Algot Blom had written to renounce his place on the course, someone else could now have it, and wouldn't it mean a lot to someone who was now without a place suddenly to be informed that, if you wish, you can come right away, there is a vacancy on the optometry course at Kongsberg. Peter had insisted. But to no avail. They couldn't be bothered to look into it any further. Finally Peter had to give up. He was, after all, a new student and reluctant to call attention to himself as a troublemaker. But there was a limit to how much he could take.

Peter related this incident in an extremely detailed and pedantic manner, making sure that not a single move he had made in his efforts to tidy things up was omitted. He was furious. With the school management, not with Algot, who was simply missing. Gone, leaving an empty place behind him, which the school would not do a damn thing to fill. Bjørn Hansen felt uncomfortable. He did not like the story Peter told, he did not like the way it was told, and he did not like what it told him about his own son and about his future prospects. He was especially worried about the latter. What would happen to his son now? The very reason why he came to Kongsberg to study optometry had disappeared. He now found himself at Kongsberg on false premises.

But Peter began his studies as if nothing serious had occurred. From now on he did not mention Algot any more. Algot was an empty place in his consciousness and he was looking to the future. Not many days passed before Bjørn Hansen regarded his son as a young man hanging on for dear life. "He hangs on for dear life." He had not liked Peter in Peter's own story. Although he tried to look on his son with all possible sympathy, he was not able to. Odd formulations constantly popped into his head, and they got stuck. Such as, "Peter eats my food, he's very welcome."

Why did he think this way? About his own son? "Peter eats my food, he's very welcome." The background to this thought was as follows: Bjørn Hansen and his son lived together in a four-room flat in the center of Kongsberg. Peter was a student at Kongsberg Engineering College and lived with his father instead of moving to a furnished room. Bjørn Hansen continued to live his regular life just as before. Peter had his own life. They saw one another only in the morning, just barely, and in the evening when Peter returned. When Peter was home he mostly stayed in his room. If he came out into the living room, it was to watch TV, which he asked, every time, whether it was all right to turn on. Breakfast, however, they had together, or at least at the same time. If Peter got up first, he went, after visiting the bathroom, into the kitchen, prepared breakfast for himself by the breadboard and put on the coffee, which was ready when his father came out to have breakfast. Sometimes they would eat at the same table, but it happened just as often that the son took his chunks of bread and a cup of coffee into his room so as to prepare himself for the day's lectures at his leisure, as he said. If the father got up first, he made coffee and sat eating at the breakfast table when his son came out and made his breakfast, before he either sat down at the table or disappeared into his own room again. But they shared the food, for Bjørn Hansen had said that it was impractical for them to buy a loaf of bread each, a bottle of milk each, etc., etc., perhaps even to use two coffee pots, as long as they happened to live in the same flat and used the same fridge and stove, to which Peter had made no objection. They had dinner separately, as it would be impractical for Peter to show up at a set hour. Besides, he obviously wanted to spend as much time as possible with his fellow students, not least eat with them—that's how you get acquainted, after all. And so Peter often ate out, in the college canteen. But it also happened that he came home in the evening without having had time to eat, as he said, and then he took a chunk of bread from the kitchen, something that happened more and more often. For that reason Bjørn Hansen began to make a double portion of his own dinner, so that his son could have the leftovers from his father's dinner when he came home. As time went by, Peter always did that, and only picked up a roll or a Danish for himself, or quite simply just a cup of coffee, when he went to the canteen for dinner with the other students. But on Sundays Peter had to manage by himself. Then Bjørn Hansen dined either with Berit and Herman Busk or at the Grand Hotel, and Peter would as a rule fry a chop, as his father could tell by the smell when he came home.

This was the way they handled the food. Nothing special or sensational about it, in a situation where a father has a son who is a student living with him. It was natural to do it that way, natural that Bjørn Hansen bought cooked meats, milk, etc., and that he prepared double portions when he made dinner, in case his son had not had dinner when he came home after a long day of lectures and study. Just as natural as his father having breakfast in the kitchen while Peter often ate in his room, so that he could prepare himself for the day's program at his leisure, and Bjørn having dinner when he was through with his working day, his son when he was through with his. All of this, in fact, betokened a good, natural relationship between father and son. The contrary would have been unnatural. That the son sat down at his father's table in spite of the fact that he really ought to have reviewed some lecture notes from yesterday, which he needed today, or that he came home for dinner at five o'clock every day. Then one might start wondering about the son. Or about the father, if he had proposed that they should share the household expenses, including the warmed-up dinners. Still, before long the father thought, "Peter eats my food, he's very welcome." Was it because deep down he was offended by Peter never suggesting they should share their household expenses? No, then Bjørn Hansen would have been offended. Was it because Peter took all of this for granted: a free room, free meals, free use of the flat's common areas? No, for Peter did not take it for granted. On the contrary, there was something about the way in which he acted toward Bjørn Hansen in such situations that hinted at duplicity, a guarded attitude.

On Sundays Bjørn Hansen dined at the Grand Hotel, when he was not at the Busks'. When he came home he noticed that his son had fried a chop or sausages and he thought, I could have invited him to the Grand with me. Originally he had intended to invite Peter to join Herman Busk and himself on their Sunday walks, then they could go to the Grand afterward, or to Herman Busk's place. But Herman Busk had already invited him: he had met Peter one day in Bjørn Hansen's flat. Then he had said that Peter was very welcome as a Sunday dinner guest, along with his father. But Peter had said that it did not suit him. He could not afford to use his Sundays for such things, he was sorry to say. A straight enough answer, in a way—a young man with an appetite for life can surely imagine better ways to spend his Sundays than to have dinner with his aging father and his aging friend and his wife. But there was something in Peter's tone that Bjørn Hansen disliked. It was so boastful. And completely devoid of the least understanding that it was his father's friend who had invited him, to show that the hospitality he gladly showed toward Bjørn Hansen would now be extended to him as well. Therefore Bjørn Hansen felt Peter's brusque declaration that he had other uses for his Sundays as a rejection not so much of Herman Busk as of himself, and in the very presence of Herman Busk, his friend, who thus had to witness how Bjørn Hansen's son refused to assume any filial obligation, despite occupying a room in his father's house.

It had sounded so unnecessary. Why could he not have given his father that pleasure? To be allowed to take along his own son to Sunday dinner at Berit and Herman Busk's house, if only once. Or he could have shown himself interested, in principle, thanked Herman Busk politely, and said he would be glad to. He didn't have to go, after all. He could have found an excuse when the time came. This episode gave Bjørn Hansen a grudge against Peter. "He hangs on for dear life," he again couldn't help thinking, without realizing in what way precisely this episode had been indicative of it. So when he perceived the smell of chops in the flat when he returned home after his dinner at the Grand, he would think, It serves him right. One day he had an errand at home before dining at the Grand. When he entered the flat, Peter was frying sausages. Sunday afternoon. He was dressed in modern leisurewear, light, loose, thin clothes, the sort young people wear when they are about to have some wholesome fun in their free time, in field and forest. He stood there in these clothes frying sausages. I won't invite him to come along, no, I won't, he can stand there with his sausage scraps. He exchanged a few words with his son and said he was going out. He was wearing his old-fashioned anorak, but Peter knew that he was off to a restaurant to have a first-class dinner; when Bjørn said he was going out, Peter knew that he was trying to hide the fact that he was going to dine out, obviously to avoid inviting him along, instead letting him stand there over his four wretched, burnt, smoked-meat sausage halves. Afterward Bjørn felt regret, of course, as he read the menu at the Grand Hotel.

Because he happened to picture Peter to himself once again. Frying sausages in the kitchen, dressed in his fashionable leisure clothes. Alone. On Sunday. Why doesn't he find someone to eat out with? he thought. It's like that every Sunday. The smell of chops hovering in the flat when he came home was a giveaway. And the lone plate in the sink. He's so much alone, he thought. There wasn't much that he knew about Peter. He knew him only from what he told him about himself and his doings when he sat down with his father to watch TV in the living room once in a while. Otherwise he saw and heard little of him, in the flat. He came back early every evening of the week.

Mostly around six or half past. If not a little past nine or a little past eleven, a little past nine, a little past eleven, the cinema having just closed; then those couple of hundred meters from Kongsberg's posh cinema straight home to Bjørn Hansen's flat. Sometimes Peter would get up from the sofa after watching TV and take a walk. But he never stayed out for long, it was just an evening stroll, or so it appeared.

Why is he not with the others? thought Bjørn. But he is, he protested to himself. On Saturdays. Then he's out till late at night. He pictured his son to himself then. Spending a long time in the bathroom before he finally comes out in his slovenly but neatly arranged young man's clothes. Sauntering past his father, sitting on the sofa, with a nonchalant toss of his head as he leaves for the Student Disco, ready to conquer life in Kongsberg on a Saturday evening in the month of October. Mingling with the others and caught up in a hectic youthfulness, until he lets himself into the flat late at night. But what about Sundays? thought Bjørn. Why is he so alone then? Why doesn't he have dinner with them then? He pictured his son to himself again. How lonely he appeared standing there. How frostily alone in all his stereotypical youthfulness. Perhaps he cannot afford to eat out with them, he thought. My son is very economical. And so he eats at home, by himself. He must have spent time with them earlier in the day. On a ramble with someone or other, and afterward, when the others go out to do things in style, returning home, because Peter is the only one who has the opportunity to make dinner at home.

For he did, after all, have contact with the others, as Bjørn Hansen could infer from the fact that Peter often mentioned several of his fellow students. As a matter of fact, even Bjørn

Hansen knew the names of more than one of them. He had noted their names because Peter had talked so much about them. Karsten Larsen who was from Nybergsund. Jan Feltskog from Skien, who had chatted up the Icelandic girl in their class, so now the two of them were sweethearts and sat at the table in the canteen with their fingers intertwined (Peter said, with a laugh). And the Swede Åke Svensson from Arvika. Not least. Bjørn Hansen had the impression that Peter and Åke, the Swede, were together continually during their study hours; in any case that they sat next to each other in class and stood side by side during the demonstrations of technical equipment at Essilov Aspit's—the country's greatest producer of optical aids (Peter had related) where much of their practical instruction took place—besides sitting at the same table as Åke in the canteen when Åke had his dinner (and Peter his coffee with perhaps a Danish), a table where also, Bjørn Hansen strongly suspected, Jan Feltskog and his sweetheart sat intertwining their fingers.

But when I come home today he'll be there, Bjørn Hansen thought. He always is. Every Sunday. And why does he never tell me who he has been hiking with? He only says he's been on a hike when I ask him what he's been doing. Doesn't Åke Svensson go hiking too? And why in the world can't they go hiking in Kongsbergmarka together, seeing how well hiking lends itself to discussing things? And they have so much to talk about, or so Bjørn Hansen had understood Peter to imply. But Peter didn't utter a word about these walks, nor about what Åke or anyone else had said or done. It doesn't have to mean that he goes hiking by himself, of course, simply because he doesn't tell me anything about it. It doesn't have to mean that. But he had begun to suspect that his son spent more time alone than was good for him.

So he was glad when Peter one day asked if he could borrow his car. A bunch of students at the engineering college were going to a rock concert in Oslo on Friday, and when it turned out that they didn't have enough cars, Peter had said he could get one. Bjørn Hansen handed over the car keys at once, elated. Not only because it was another indication that his suspicion that Peter merely wandered about by himself, like a weirdo, was completely unfounded, but also because, by asking if he could borrow the car, he acted as a "son" toward him, instead of only seeing him as a benevolent landlord, which he often had a feeling Peter was doing, a situation he simply had to put up with, without being able to do anything about it one way or the other, because it was so difficult for Bjørn to open up after such a long separation from his son. Peter drove away and, with four students crammed into his father's old jalopy, set off for the rock concert in the capital, a journey of about an hour and a half each way.

In the morning, Peter handed back the keys over breakfast and Bjørn Hansen asked how the concert had been. "Good," Peter said. "But it became expensive. Because I filled up the tank, and when we got back to Kongsberg and we were to settle, they refused to pay up. Every one of them. After I had been chauffeuring them all evening, and they had been drinking beer after beer once the concert was over, while I was sitting there with a soft drink. And then they even refused to pay their share."—"Why?" Bjørn Hansen asked. Peter shrugged. "Don't know," he said, "they made a joke of it."

So, Peter didn't know why his friends refused to club together for the petrol. They had made a joke of it. Bjørn Hansen would have given a lot to know in what way they had found it funny, but he could not ask and his son was unwilling to elaborate. But he became outraged. It was a rotten thing to do and quite unusual, or so he assumed. What was there about his son that made it possible for three friends to treat a fourth friend in that way? Were they such good friends that the joke quite simply was a joke, it being understood that next time Karsten would drive and Peter would be a passenger, and then Karsten would pay for petrol and be the chauffeur of the evening, with only a soft drink to console himself with?

"But then I threw them out," Peter said, in his usual too loud voice. "They damn well had to walk home, and Halvor Mørk had at least four kilometers to walk, but walk he must since he wouldn't pay. You see, I had stopped at the marketplace just to settle up before taking them home, one after the other. It was in the middle of the night, damn it, four o'clock in the morning, and now they thought that, after acting as their trusty chauffeur, I would take them home, too, without them even paying for the petrol! Well, they crawled out then, hurried toward the taxi stand and took a taxi home—at least Halvor did. What the others did I don't know, but in any case, the taxi cost more than they would have had to pay me for the petrol." Bjørn Hansen felt uncomfortable. He did not like the situation. This was no ordinary joke, this was something quite different. There were three of them against Peter, three fellow students against his son. Why didn't they want to pay for the petrol, but would rather take a taxi? It was not a matter of money, but something else. But what? Why did they treat his son like that, after Peter had offered to get a car and thereby solve a difficult problem for them, then drive them to and from Oslo, besides having to sit around and wait, so to speak, while his friends took the opportunity to have a night out in the capital, once they happened to be there?

Don't overreact, Bjørn Hansen told himself. Take it easy. This is only an unfortunate episode, for which Peter must take most of the blame. They were just four friends going to a rock concert in Oslo together, and Peter offered to drive. Next time it may be Karsten, or the third one, that fellow Halvor Mørk. This was understood, as a presupposition, and therefore the three others thought it was rather clumsy of Peter to start pestering them about payment at four o'clock in the morning—just think, getting out wallets, digging out notes and coins, a great fuss with change, no, drive us home, Peter, we'll take care of this later, hell, yes! Surely, that was how it must have been: a very pleasant evening that ended rather stupidly because Peter can, in truth, be a bit difficult and clumsy socially, as I have noticed many times, Bjørn Hansen thought. And besides, Peter did not seem crushed, only slightly annoyed. And in the evening he went out, to the Student Pub, and returned late at night, since it was Saturday.

Although—late at night? For once Bjørn noted the time when he was awoken by Peter letting himself in. 12:35. The following Saturday he woke up in the same way. He heard his son come in and tiptoe through the flat. He looked at the time. Almost 12:30. The Saturday after that he also woke up. He didn't feel like looking at the clock, but he looked anyway. He shouldn't have bothered. It was 12:35. That is to say, when he had been out having a good time his son came home at 12:35. It was not especially "late at night." In fact, it's the earliest a young man can in decency return home after being out having a good time on Saturday night.

Bjørn Hansen understood. He could no longer deny it. This

was the proof. He had a son who nobody wanted to spend time with, no more than was strictly necessary at any rate. His son's footsteps at 12:35 on Saturday night, so regular that you could set your watch by them, testified to that. *And he knows it himself*. That was the worst part. Otherwise one could say it didn't matter. He's trying to hide it, not least from me, Bjørn Hansen thought. "Good Lord!" he burst out. But Bjørn Hansen now knew. That his son was friendless. Evidently there was nobody who liked him very much.

Not even Algot, the friend whom Peter had described as his good genius. Who Peter had stuck with through thick and thin in the army. Oh sure, Algot must have let Peter stick with him through thick and thin, and so his son had wanted to study the same as Algot, and in the same school, so he could continue to be allowed to stick with him through thick and thin. Yes, Peter had dreamed about sticking with Algot through thick and thin for his whole life, as Algot Blom's trusted shop manager. But Algot hadn't even bothered to inform him that he had changed his mind. And so Peter sucks up to some classmates who are going to a rock concert in Oslo. Tempts them by saying he can provide a car and drive them, as their chauffeur, back and forth, which they allow him most graciously to do, relieving them of any further worries about transport. But when the fellow demands that they *pay* for it, that's the limit. 12:35. Always letting himself in at 12:35.

The worst thing was that his father understood them. The others. There was something about his son that inspired dislike. His voice alone—it was far too loud. He spoke over people's heads. Bjørn could vividly imagine his son in the Engineering School canteen, with his everlasting Danish and cup of coffee as he enlarged on the fact that *he* dined at home and thereby saved money, which the others had to listen to as they ate. In all likelihood they had seen him coming, with his cup of coffee and Danish on a plate, hoping that he would sit at another table. It's just too damn bad, thought Bjørn. All that my son is doing, after all, is following a natural urge to be part of the ordinary social life of young students. And he was perfectly welcome to do so, but preferably not at their table.

From now on Bjørn Hansen began to feel pain whenever his son spoke with enthusiasm about his own times. It hurt to listen to Peter's explanations of the hectic rhythm of the times, not least the condescending tone in which he addressed Bjørn Hansen, because Bjørn Hansen knew better. But Peter didn't know that Bjørn Hansen knew, so he continued as before. He spoke with enthusiasm about his own times, out there. About the volume of the electrified howl in the basement room, an almost sacred sound. About the determination of his cohort of students, the new stalwarts of optometry, who refused to let themselves be trampled on, but would turn the practical application of optics into something quite different from what it is today, as little by little they would begin to operate all over Norway, not to mention the rest of the Nordic countries. It pained Bjørn Hansen's soul to hear Peter discuss his fellow students with great friendliness, indeed, often with admiration. About living here at Kongsberg, under the neon-lit sign of CITY, a civilization, highly technological at that, in the middle of the rock pile that is Norway. About the fact that our times are merciless, casting out those who don't move with them, and rightly so. Here again Peter Korpi Hansen was thinking about young people who had thoughtlessly thrown themselves into yesterday's fashionable studies and would find the door slammed in their faces when they went to look for a job afterward. But with an education from the only school in the Northern countries that trained opticians, one was in the front rank. Peter didn't make a secret of how smart he was, and how this had led him to enroll in the optometry program at Kongsberg Engineering College, although he admitted that he had been very close to going to Volda, where he would now be studying media. Yes, that's what could have happened. Chance often prevails. "But not all the time," he added furiously. "Because as soon as I was directed into optics, I said goodbye to any thought of media studies. I had no doubt about what was the right thing," he said, and Bjørn Hansen once more had to hear his son's gloating voice fill the living room of his flat, drowning out the TV, which was also on.

In such instances Bjørn Hansen could not help wondering what would have happened had Peter known that his father knew how things really were with his son. To Bjørn's surprise it struck him that it would have made no difference. Peter would have said exactly the same thing, in the same tone of voice, still gloating over the same details. This young man, who was superfluous and cast off, was in fact genuinely enthusiastic about precisely his own times and his peers, with whom he cultivated a fellowship, in clothes, music, social tone, and dreams. "But you're so lonely, my son," Bjørn Hansen could have said, to which his son would have smiled patronizingly. Lonely. "Certainly," he would have said. "That's the way of youth. Haven't you heard our music? The solidarity it creates among us is, after all, based on the fact that it can openly express the damn loneliness which is at the bottom of every modern soul. We can fling it loudly into space, like a resounding howl, and spew it up the wall," Bjørn Hansen thought Peter might answer then. "In fact, it's quite natural for a young man to be lonely, Dad," he would have added, Bjørn Hansen thought; but he instantly felt a pang, for he had noticed that during the two months his son had lived with him, he had never heard him conclude a sentence addressed to Bjørn Hansen with "Dad." But then Bjørn Hansen could have confronted him with the fact that the other students refused, after all, to have anything to do with him if they could avoid it. He could have mentioned the episode when Peter had driven a few of them to and from Oslo and how they had ridiculed him for being brazen enough to demand that they should club together on the petrol, as if they were a bunch of friends who had gone to Oslo together. That, too, Peter could have answered: "OK, it's true, that originally they hadn't meant to take me along. And that they became interested only when I mentioned that I could borrow your car. But so what? It's often that way in life. You have to use the means at your disposal. I used your car and offered to drive them. Does that mean I'm a "hanger-on"? Maybe, but I felt like being a "hanger-on." Still, I won't put up with anything whatsoever just because I have to be a hanger-on and wouldn't get asked otherwise. One day I will be asked in another way. But while I wait for that, they damn well have to put up with paying for the petrol." That is how he imagined Peter might have answered, loudly and preachily. He was enlightening his father about perfectly natural ways of behaving in a given situation, it was as simple as that. Yes, Peter could have explained everything, pointing out that it was an episode experienced in his own times by a young man who, entirely unaffected, shook it off and carried on. The only question that Bjørn Hansen was unable to imagine Peter giving an answer to was 12:35.

In a way it was almost a relief, for the answers he put into Peter's mouth chimed all too well with the way Peter was, so that his son's reticence, aloofness and, yes, embarrassment at being confronted every Saturday with having to let himself into the flat and stealing through the living room without waking his father or, if his father awoke all the same, Peter knowing for certain that it was, after all, well past midnight, reconciled Bjørn in some way to his own son. His despair at his son being disliked and rejected by his peers was then countered by Peter's embarrassment at having been exposed in his freezing loneliness, and this led to a reconciliation with his own son which he otherwise had difficulty achieving—well, even here he achieved it only in his imagination, indeed, at the extreme edge of his imagination.

For he was not certain that he liked his only son, that is, the only thing that would be left after him, in the end. Though he was in despair about Peter's incurable loneliness, which only expressed itself in his son's stolen steps across the living-room floor at 12:35 every Saturday night, he understood all too well its cause. He couldn't endure his son's preachy and boastful manner. It revolted him, although what Peter expressed in this way was his enthusiasm for his own times, which Bjørn had to allow him, of course, in addition to the fact that it showed his son was prepared to fight hard for the life that was, after all, his own, chillingly his own, Bjørn Hansen might add. It was Peter's spark of life that manifested itself in this way, what would be left after him, that is, in his own flesh and blood, in the genes, which would blindly push on, in as yet unborn lives. But there was something about this spark of life that frightened him. A sneaky air Peter had. In his relationship with his father. As if he were constantly saying, "Don't even try! You can't buy me back as your son, in this house I'm a tenant and you're my landlord." There was a distance in everything Peter did which expressed this. Nevertheless, he could not resist the temptation to gain advantage from being Bjørn Hansen's only son, and in such a way that Bjørn felt certain Peter crowed over it among his fellow students. He was afraid he might offend his son by acting in such a way that Peter was bound to perceive it as an overture to him in his capacity as a father. Make him feel irritated or troubled. There were so many things he would have given him, but held back because he feared Peter would interpret it as pressure to make him come out as a "son." That underhanded air of his every time he accepted something, like his meals, which his father had arranged so that he could eat without having to play the role of "son," suggested a strong, distinctive spark of life in him, which Bjørn nevertheless could never quite resign himself to, because it was without generosity (But how many young men are generous? They can only latch on to their own future!) and without a sense of shame (and he expected to find a sense of shame in a young man), which, he had to admit, also manifested itself in another distinct manner, namely, the pushiness that Peter's fellow students had experienced and tried to bear with, however grudgingly. Peter was going to be an optician. He spoke about the high level of competency placed at one's disposal by the Kongsberg Engineering College in this field, as though it were a prize he had pocketed on account of his ability. But the subject itself occupied him very little. He was only mildly interested in optical science, which was, after all, what he was here to learn about. He regarded it as pretty much the price he had to pay to get an education with a future. Bjørn had wondered why Peter, with his good marks, hadn't looked for another field of study, choosing to become a doctor or an engineer, but that was clearly far from his mind, he showed no ambition at all in that direction. Algot did not explain everything, for if Peter had joined the army with a clear ambition to be a physician, an engineer or a lawyer, even Algot could not have made him choose to be an optician instead. It had been media versus optics, and there Peter had, to his own crowing satisfaction, chosen correctly, namely optics. This decision might seem rather questionable to outsiders, and Peter's own cocksureness all but incomprehensible. After all, media means power. The new breed of visual and literary scholars, who by virtue of their knowledge can exploit the secret language of the TV screen must, after all, have had a seductive effect on Peter. Nonetheless, he chose to be an optician. To remedy the weaknesses of the eye with the help of optical science. It was unthinkable that he would have made this choice without Algot's influence, but the strange thing was that he had made this choice at all. Algot's influence must have been greater than Peter's dream of belonging to that select group of modern media experts, with their power and adventurous lifestyles, as opposed to the rather sedentary life in the back room of an optician's shop, albeit dressed in a white smock. But there, in the back room of the optician's shop, Peter Korpi Hansen was to leave his imprint on existence, as someone who fully understood it. That was his goal. Algot did not come. Optics as a subject was of little interest to Peter. He could have left. The premises for his remaining weren't there, after all. But he remained. His classmates disliked him, just barely tolerated that he sat down at their table in the canteen. But in the evening he would sit and talk enthusiastically to his father about Kongsberg Engineering College, about its wonderful student life, the pulse of the times, visiting lecturers who came from NIT and were at their beck and call, and about his great fellow students, among whom Åke Svensson from Arvika, in particular, stood high in his favor. For Peter had found his niche. He had found the means by which he would put his own stamp on existence.

According to Peter it was Åke, the Swede, who had suggested the idea to him. "Here we are, forty of us," he had said, "and, afterward, which one do the customers prefer? The best one, naturally. But we are all the best, from the customer's viewpoint. After three years here we can all do the technical part of the job to the full satisfaction of the customer. We've all learned that much. After all, every one of us can find the correct lens for any eye whatsoever and can identify those who have diseased eyes and send them to an oculist. Even those of us who slept in class when the eye specialist was here will have picked up enough to enable them to distinguish a diseased eye from one that simply has impaired vision. Our domain is the eye with impaired vision, and everyone will be able to provide the correct eyeglass or lens for it. For those whom we shall serve, we will all be equally capable. That one is better than another is obvious only to opticians. All the same, the customers will prefer one optician to another. Some will be successful, others will struggle. Who will be a success when, in reality, we are all equally capable? The one who can offer something different, of course. The one who can offer beauty," Åke said. "The fashionable pair of glasses."

This had made an enormous impression on Bjørn Hansen's son, who did not even dream about owning his own optician's shop, but of being an assistant to Algot Blom, or someone like him. It was by interpreting the whims of fashion that an optician distinguished himself. Applying the whims of fashion quite concretely to a particular pair of glasses. Realizing that this was where the future lay for an optician. Peter had understood that. But it was Åke who had given him the idea. For that he would be eternally grateful to Åke Svensson, he said. For his having planted these words in him. Words that Peter hid in his heart and brooded on, for Bjørn Hansen understood that Peter could very well expatiate enthusiastically on what this really meant in the presence of his father, but never when he was in the company of his fellow students. Then he listened and kept quiet. Because now he was at the cutting edge, he had seen what it was all about. He had to learn his métier, of course. But in addition to that, one had to understand the time one lived in. Its whims, which are the innermost essence of time.

Bjørn Hansen watched his son. He could imagine him as an optician. An assistant in an optician's. He could not imagine him as a lawyer, doctor, or engineer. Or working in the media, whether in advertising, film, or as a TV presenter. He had found his niche in life. A profession that really meant nothing to him, which he had chosen by chance and on the assumption that it assured his future, because there were few opticians in relation to the demand, as opposed to the media where too many are called. His son as an optician. As he comes up with the right pair of glasses for his client. Displaying a gloating pride as he plunges his hand straight into his own time and in an almost mysterious way pulls out a pair of glasses that is perfectly adapted to the shape of the client's face, viewed in the light of the time's changing expressiveness or staunch conformity. This was not only his son, but it was his son's dream and the quivering goal of his existence.

It was clear that the idea he had picked up from Åke, the Swede, released something in Peter. It could not be denied that he had studied at random, because the foundation of his efforts had vanished before he had begun. He had read diligently, that's true, but without any special purpose. Apart, perhaps, from a hope, far back in his head, that a letter would arrive from Algot in which everything would be explained and remedied. He had read to kill time. But now he could look ahead to the day when he had finished his studies, in two and a half years, and a future that was no longer dependent on a friend who had betrayed him in such an incomprehensible way. He was as lonely as before, but showed it less, except, of course, at the hour when loneliness struck, between 11:30 and 12:35, when he understood that he had once again been de trop among his peers, one must assume.

The end of the autumn term was approaching, Peter would soon be going home, to Narvik, for Christmas. Since they shared the flat, Bjørn had discovered what it felt like to have a modern young man living with him. For example, from the bathroom being occupied when he had to use it. And from the fact that the scent from his son's perfumes, body lotion, after-shave, stick deodorant and shampoo hovered in the air when at last he could go in there, drowning out the more primitive smell from his son's insides, which was only imperceptibly present, like an evaporated, unidentifiable token of his son's hairy presence. Bjørn saw him leave in the morning, nonchalant, self-assured, dressed for battle in the very costume of youth. And come back in the evening, or in the late afternoon, and warm up the dinner in the microwave that Bjørn Hansen had bought in preparation for his son coming to live with him. Then Peter went to his own room to study, or perhaps rest. But he came out into the living room again, sat down on the sofa and talked. About his pet subject. He took pleasure in putting down the other students. Those who failed to understand that opticians should take part in the general enlightenment of the masses. Those who thought the only important thing was to acquire some elementary knowledge about the relationship between the shape of a person's face and the chosen frame and lenses. He didn't even refrain from putting down Åke. Åke who had given him the idea, but had failed to understand the substance of what he himself had said. He had taken it to be a stray thought, an amusing detail to be trifled with, though half in earnest. But not in deadly earnest. Like Peter. "Huge lenses for a woman with a long face," he said, laughing. "That's obvious. For then the woman's face becomes soft. They think all they have to do is to learn such elementary rules. But what if the woman's face doesn't need to be soft? Doesn't this softness expected of women seem a trifle banal? After all, emphasizing the hardness of a woman's long face might make it sparkle in a mysterious, provocative way. Pure and hard. Square specs, with low lenses, for her." The direct opposite, in fact, of what was taught, which his fellow students took to be eternal truths. "There are no eternal truths, only a hectic rhythm of life, situations in which people have a chance to shine, so that the situation is the firmament and the perfect people its stars," Peter said solemnly and with great and genuine pathos. Oh, if only his son could have spoken with such emotion about optical science instead! About the knowledge which would enable him to work with the lens's curvatures to arrive at –2.5 and –1.7. This scanty knowledge, however, could not raise his son's mind to the great heights and prepare his encounter with real life. And that was what Peter was now talking about, preaching about, to his father. Preaching and preaching. About life and his own future, to which his eyes had now been opened. Before it had only been life, the admirable life of his own times. Now he also knew how *he* would function within it. His eyes had been opened. He talked and talked. In the same monotonous, all too loud voice. Over his father's head, but straight in his ears. Bjørn got an earful. The whole thing had developed very differently to the way he had imagined. Bjørn Hansen had been waiting all through autumn for Peter to "attack" him. Why had he abandoned his only son when he was just two years old? Didn't he know it meant that a whole facet of existence had been lost to him, the son? Bjørn also waited for Peter to tell him that he hadn't visited him since he was fourteen years old because he had expected his father to reveal himself and ask him, urgently, to come down anyway, since he couldn't bear the thought of losing him. But Peter never made any such "attack" on him. Not with a word did he refer to what had been between them. Not with a word, not with a look did he hint at anything that could have turned Peter into Bjørn Hansen's "son," and Bjørn, consequently, into Peter's "father." The "attack" never came. But Bjørn Hansen had been waiting. He had prepared his answer. That he regretted nothing, and therefore couldn't make any overture that might turn him into Peter's "father" and, accordingly, Peter into his own "son." For he couldn't make use of the word "regret," knowing that he would have acted exactly the same if given a second chance. With that he had lost his son, and Peter was the only one who could remedy the situation, if he wanted to. But Peter did not. He had no idea what his father was talking about. He couldn't care less about the whole thing. Instead, Peter talked about the enthusiasm he felt for his own brilliant epoch and its enlightened people, to which he was fully entitled. There was a curse on the relationship between father and son. Evening after evening, the lonely young man preached to his father about life out there, in the future. With his naked young face, which had Bjørn Hansen's own features, Peter explained self-confidently how he would fix the future. How he would get so close to it, so close that he could grasp it, from the modest fancied position he occupied as trusted manager of Algot Blom's main branch in Oslo, or wherever he would end up—it being not at all certain that he would end up at Algot Blom's, there being so many possibilities. This he could boastfully, for the first time, tell his father, in confidence. Bjørn Hansen was listening. He was rather reserved as he sat there, getting an earful. He only said, "You don't say?—Well—you think so?—Oh really?—That might be worth thinking about." But it didn't affect Peter. He talked and talked. Enthusiastically and monotonously, in his too loud voice. Bjørn Hansen wished he would stop. He couldn't bear to listen to any more testimony about the modern world, to which his son was so proud of belonging heart and soul. With all its stylishness and elegance, which Peter had now latched on to by interpreting the modernity of his own life in such a way that he could create a truly astonishing spectacle frame, one that would make people gasp with admiration. But his son didn't stop. He talked and talked. In the morning as well, even before Bjørn Hansen was fully awake and had managed to prepare himself for another day, his son would stand at the pull-out breadboard by the countertop cutting his slices of bread, while talking boastfully about the pulse of the age to which he belonged and the importance of understanding it. "With his obscenely naked face," "like your spitting image," rigged out in a costume from his plentiful and label-laden wardrobe, he stood there, self-assured and self-indulgent, preaching to Bjørn Hansen about the superiority of his own times, which he was a part of, not apart from, before he took his cup of coffee and his slices of bread and went into his own room, so that his father could finally settle down and have breakfast in peace and quiet. At the same time Bjørn felt a stab of bad conscience.

For perhaps I misunderstand it all, he thought. Perhaps this is a communication from a "son." Perhaps this is "the voice of the son." A young man who opens his heart to his father about the journey he has set out on and the adventures that await him out there. A message, that is, which he brings from out there, to his father. If that was the case, did his voice signify that the one who opened his heart was his father's heir, the one who would carry life onward? Was Peter letting him know how he would seize the torch? Possibly, possibly. However preachy his manner, it was perhaps a "son" who spoke, far away, but still perhaps a "son." Who spoke to him. Who tried to reach him, as a son. Bjørn Hansen felt moved, and uneasy. For was there not in this communication also—if it really did come from his "son"—a tacit inquiry, well, a secret hope, that his father, far down there, had to offer him his recognition? A small spark? Which was to be kindled between the two of them? Was it possible that Peter had done so? Something Peter certainly could do, but which he himself had forfeited the possibility of doing. Was he trying to make himself known now? Not in the form of an "attack," which he had waited for and waited for several months on end, but in this highly surprising way? Suddenly it dawned on Bjørn Hansen that his son, who had talked and talked in his preachy fashion, self-confidently and boastfully, and in a patronizing tone, had perhaps really been saying all the time, again and again, "Say something to me, Dad. Recognize me for what I am, recognize the life I'm going to live and that I'm preparing myself for. Do that, Dad." Could it be possible that he had a son who for several months, from the very moment he had come to Kongsberg and settled in as a guest in his father's flat, had asked, time and again, for a word of recognition? Yes, it was possible. Was this really a "son" who was trying to call attention to his own life and his life's purpose, in order to get recognition from his "father"? Astonished, Bjørn Hansen had to admit that one could not discount that possibility. And if that were the case, then he could, by giving this recognition, become Peter's father in Peter's own eyes and consequently be reunited with his son. He could say the redeeming word, with the result that the curse that stood between them would lose its efficacy. But even if this were the case, it was nevertheless no use. It could just as well be the exact opposite. For he could not give Peter this recognition. It was that simple and shocking. Peter could only talk and talk. And continue to preach at him, in his too loud voice, which changed nothing. My poor orphan son, he thought.

Christmas was coming to Kongsberg too. Peter had a kind of mock exam just before the holidays, and when it was over he packed and went home to Narvik to celebrate there. He had only one suitcase with him when he left, and his father accompanied him to the station. The train arrived, and Bjørn held out his hand to him. "I'll be back," Peter said. "After Christmas. It's so nice staying with you." His father smiled and wished him a pleasant journey. You'll be back after Christmas, he thought. But you won't stay for very long. That I know.

Christmas came. Bjørn Hansen celebrated Christmas quietly, all alone, only interrupted by dinner at Berit and Herman Busk's the second day of Christmas, as usual. Peter returned at the beginning of January, and in the middle of that same month Bjørn Hansen left for Vilnius. Where is Vilnius? Vilnius is situated somewhere or other in Europe. It is impossible to state it more precisely. You take the train from Kongsberg to Oslo, fly from Fornebu to Kastrup in Copenhagen, and after an hour's wait in the transit hall you board a plane bound for Vilnius. After a flight of an hour and twenty minutes, you land in the airport of Lithuania's capital. Then you are one hundred and twenty miles from Minsk, if you travel in an easterly direction. Riga is one hundred and eighty miles to the northwest, Warsaw two hundred and forty miles south. It is four hundred miles to St. Petersburg, five hundred and fifty to Moscow, and five hundred and twenty miles to Berlin. Midway between Berlin and Moscow, somewhere in Europe. To the Baltic coast, with Lithuania's most important seaport, Klaipeda, and to the bathing resorts, it is one hundred and fifty miles.

So Bjørn Hansen found himself in Vilnius. He was staring out of the window of his room on the eighteenth floor of the typical Soviet-Russian Hotel Lithuania, down at the city on the other side of the river Neris. An old, venerable city. In Europe. A castle rose proudly on the top of a hill, together with Gedimina's tower, and below it lay the city with its churches, buildings, towers and walls. Bjørn Hansen was moved by the view from the window and decided to go out at once. Shortly afterward he was crossing a stone bridge over to the other side of the river, where the old city was located. A city with a skeleton from the thirteen hundreds. A centuries-old home for Lithuanians, Poles, White Russians and Jews. Now a Lithuanian population with a large Russian minority. A place with narrow cobbled streets and a smell of coke. With smoke rising and settling on the city. A smell of coke and rancid cooking oil. Bjørn Hansen hurrying through the streets in his western clothes, quite drab by Norwegian standards. Everyone looked at him. They stood watching him from cramped courtyards. In their worn, old-fashioned clothes. With bundles under their arms. Bent over and hunchbacked. But they observed him with eyes shining with curiosity. He was an envoy from America. Cabbage and potatoes. Rolls of fabric in the shops lining the streets. A man pulling a cart full of empty milk bottles. It rattles. Bjørn Hansen hurried along, actually feeling rather uncomfortable. The old city gate, from the 1500s. St. Kasimir Church. A theater from the 1700s. The palace of the archbishops. The new City Hall, from the 1700s. The university, from the 1500s, with St. John Church. The Gedimina Square with the cathedral and the freestanding bell tower. Ding-dong. It was cold and he shivered. It was the middle of winter. People were hurrying through the narrow streets. Suddenly it began to snow. It was such a dark day in Vilnius, and suddenly it began to snow. Yes, here, in this city, Bjørn Hansen got to see it snow in Central European fashion. The snow fell wet and heavy upon Vilnius, which long ago was called Lithuania's Jerusalem and between the wars was a Polish provincial town.

Large white snowflakes in the air, which came floating down, got sucked up by the ground and evaporated. The snow fell in heavy white flakes between the baroque buildings, over the tortuous narrow streets, down on the people's padded shoulders and into their hair, wetting it. All at once the streets were full of schoolchildren, who tried to catch the snowflakes in the air. They suddenly entered the street from small, narrow openings in the row of houses, dressed in school uniforms and carrying their books in slings, which they hastened to get rid of by putting them on cornices, into niches in the walls, or onto stairs, before they ran into the middle of the street to catch the snow with their eager hands. They clapped as they caught the snow in the air, at a quick pace, in the vain hope of catching enough snowflakes to make a snowball. Bjørn Hansen hurried on through the city while observing this strange sudden scene which unfolded so spontaneously before his eyes. He again came to the old stone bridge across the river Neris and to his secluded hotel, Lithuania, which throned it on the other side.

He shook the melted snow from his hair as he stepped into the reception of Hotel Lithuania. The reception was deep and dark, in a pompous style of the 1960s. Thick carpets on the floor, dim lighting, with, at the very end, a long reception desk with twinkling small lights. In front of it stood a party of people, who were jovially greeting another party with hugs and exaggerated gestures. Bjørn Hansen hurried up, because he knew the people who made up one of the parties. It was the party to which he, too, belonged and they were now greeting their Lithuanian hosts. For Bjørn Hansen was in Vilnius as a member of a delegation. He had been handpicked for a Norwegian delegation of municipal civil servants bound for

Lithuania for the purpose of teaching the Lithuanians democracy. And now, here they were, greeting those who were to be taught. They would have discussions and conversations with Lithuanians who were selected to fill important positions in the local administration of this ex-Soviet republic, which had now declared its independence. The object was for the Norwegians to give the Lithuanians some good advice on how local democracy can function in a sensible way, so that the local population can both be governed and take part in the governing. It was not unreasonable that such a delegation would take along a Norwegian town treasurer, nor that this Norwegian treasurer was Bjørn Hansen, because, after all, he had served as such for almost twenty years, and had also during that time held several positions of trust within the Association of Norwegian City and Borough Treasurers.

The conference, which began immediately after these introductions in the vestibule, took place in the very hotel where the Norwegians were staying. There followed three more days of meetings, interrupted by sightseeing in Vilnius and a day trip around and about in Lithuania. The last evening featured a festive dinner, whereupon the Norwegian delegation returned to Oslo. Bjørn Hansen had little to say about the conference itself. He must have felt rather indisposed, both because of abundant partying in the evenings and his own thoughts. But he noticed, from the very start, that this meeting between Norwegian and Lithuanian municipal administrators had a peculiar air about it. The Norwegians were idolized. More so than he actually cared to be, because what they were idolized for was not their own worth as individuals but their desirable nationality.

The Lithuanians were dreaming they were in Bjørn Hansen's shoes. They looked upon his shoes as extremely elegant and even pointed at them. And as a result Bjørn Hansen felt it was strange to find himself in his own shoes. His watch, too, had a promising aura about it. They looked upon the person wearing it as someone who manifested a natural superiority. Every now and then he was asked what time it was, even though the Lithuanians had their own watches. Then Bjørn Hansen extended his arm, looked at his wristwatch and gave the time the dial showed, in German. But the Lithuanians were not listening, they just *looked*, spellbound, at what was revealed on Bjørn Hansen's wrist as he jerked his shirtsleeve back so that his watch came into sight, a natural movement he had made thousands of times previously without it causing any commotion whatsoever. And these were not ignorant people from the Lithuanian countryside, the direct descendants of dumb serfs. They were well-educated people who had been selected to be local leaders in the new Lithuania. They represented the backbone of the new Lithuania. And Bjørn Hansen was not the only one who became the object of their endless admiration simply because he walked about in his own clothes. The entire Norwegian delegation experienced the same thing. And since they were rather sober, some might say rather gray, Norwegian municipal bosses, few of whom, if any, could be said to be smartly dressed, it was not surprising that the mood of the Norwegian delegation became quite elated, and inevitably many of them felt extremely flattered. For Bjørn Hansen, however, it led him to understand that the plan he had come to Lithuania to carry out could not fail.

Therefore he left the hotel before breakfast on the second day and hailed a taxi. He was anxious but calm. He asked the taxi to take him to the largest hospital in Vilnius. The problem was to find the right man; if he did, everything would go like clockwork. Dr. Schiøtz had given him some good advice as to how he should proceed, what kind of specialist he should look for, and how high up the hospital hierarchy he should go, and when the taxi stopped outside a gigantic hospital complex, he managed, with the help of a German-Lithuanian dictionary, to find his way to Dr. Lustinvas.

He told Dr. Lustinvas that although his request might appear rather strange to him, he still asked permission to fully explain why he had sought him out. Dr. Lustinvas nodded, inviting him to speak. He was a man of about thirty, dressed the way doctors dress everywhere in the world, in a white coat. Bjørn Hansen presented his request. Not once while he related what services he wanted the doctor to carry out did Dr. Lustinvas show any sign of emotion. He neither gaped nor raised his eyebrows. Even though it must have seemed completely insane to him, he appeared quite unmoved; rather indifferent, in fact. It didn't matter to him. He listened, and when Bjørn Hansen had finished Dr. Lustinvas gave a shrug and said that, if it really were true that Mr. Hansen wanted this, he could not see that there existed any serious obstacle to having it done. But, he added, naturally such an operation could not be undertaken for free, something Mr. Hansen must surely understand. The only thing he wondered about was whether Mr. Hansen realized that he would have to pay the fee in cash, so he sincerely hoped that Mr. Hansen had borne that in mind when he left his native country to come here, and had taken the necessary measures in advance. When Bjørn Hansen confirmed this, Dr. Lustinvas nodded, showing thereby that he was satisfied with his new patient. But when Bjørn Hansen mentioned the sum he had expected to pay, Dr. Lustinvas gave a start. Had he heard correctly? Was it possible? Was this man from the West offering him $10,000? For barely anything at all? Dr. Lustinvas repeated the sum:

$10, 000? In cash? Bjørn Hansen confirmed it. Dr. Lustinvas rose and gave Bjørn Hansen his hand. He was visibly moved, and although he tried to hide it, he didn't quite manage to. Dr. Lustinvas's hand trembled.

At the end of this conversation, after Bjørn Hansen had paid an advance of $1,000 and they had arranged what happened next at their leisure, Bjørn Hansen could return to the Hotel Lithuania and the conference. He came back just in time for lunch. No one found it strange that he had been away in the morning, because the night before had been pretty boozy and the Lithuanian participants in particular gave him a jolly welcome when he finally turned up. Thereafter he participated fully in the remainder of the conference, both in the meetings, the sightseeing tours, the dinners and the rest of the partying, while he kept hidden the fact that his thoughts were elsewhere. He drank moderately, but made the most of what little he drank in an exceedingly drunken manner. After a festive dinner in the hotel's assembly hall on the last evening, the festivities continued in the bar and the adjacent room. The time had come to swear eternal friendship, and Bjørn Hansen gladly drank a toast to his new friends. He was invited up to the room of one of the Lithuanians in order to continue the fraternal celebrations with a number of others, something he would not have turned down under normal circumstances. But now he said he would drop by a little later. He had to get a breath of fresh air first. He said this with a crooked smile and in a slightly snuffling voice, which made the others understand that, indeed, he needed some fresh air straightaway. Then he put on his overcoat, handed in his key at reception, as is the custom, and stepped out into the late January evening. When he knew he could no longer be seen from the hotel, he straightened his back and strolled through the streets with firm, relaxed steps. It was snowing. The same snow as before. Heavy white snowflakes upon the sparsely illuminated European city of Vilnius. He reached the hospital, where Dr. Lustinvas stood on the stairs to receive him.

He was led into the hospital and taken, via some back stairs, to a room with a bed. This was his room, a private room. Dr. Lustinvas left him alone while he got ready. He undressed and hung his clothes in a tall wardrobe in the austerely furnished room. Then he lay down on the bed. After a while Dr. Lustinvas entered, accompanied by two nurses. Under Dr. Lustinvas's supervision, Bjørn Hansen was bandaged and put in plaster according to the medical rules that applied to a case of this kind.

It gave rise to concern when Bjørn Hansen did not show up the next morning. Neither at breakfast, nor when the Norwegian delegation gathered at reception to leave for the airport. Nor was his suitcase among the Norwegian delegation's luggage, which had been brought together at reception and was watched over by a cloakroom attendant. An inquiry at the reception desk yielded the information that the key which Bjørn Hansen had handed in the previous evening had not been picked up again. When they let themselves into his room, they found it empty, but with his things still there. They called the airport and had him paged, in case, for some obscure reason or other, he had gone straight there without bothering to take his luggage. They were now beginning to be seriously concerned. The bus to the airport was already waiting, but no Bjørn Hansen could be tracked down. Then a very upset member of the Lithuanian delegation pulled the leader of the Norwegian delegation aside. He had received a message from the hospital to the effect that Bjørn Hansen had been admitted after a traffic accident, and had been operated on for his injuries. His condition was serious but not life-threatening. What now? The plane would soon leave and it was time to get to the airport. But could they just take off and leave Bjørn Hansen behind in a Lithuanian hospital seriously injured? Maybe one or two of them should stay and give him support? The Lithuanian delegation leader assured them that this was not necessary. First, it wouldn't do him much good for a long time and, second, he was in the best of hands. In case anything came up, the embassy in Warsaw had already been notified. An embassy secretary would visit him as soon as the time was ripe. This soothed the Norwegian delegation sufficiently to persuade them to leave for home together at the appointed time.

Bjørn Hansen remained in Vilnius Hospital for several weeks. He was Dr. Lustinvas's patient and nobody else was allowed near him without Dr. Lustinvas's permission. Sometimes Dr. Lustinvas visited him with some other doctors, who would stand in the middle of the room: he could hear Dr. Lustinvas speaking to them in an undertone. Or else Dr. Lustinvas would pay a call accompanied by a flock of nurses, one after another, like a little procession, in which case the visit with the envoy from the West was only part of an all-inclusive round of visits. Once a day a nurse came to change his bandages and to rub him thoroughly with ointments. Two nurses took turns at it, the same ones who had bandaged him and put him in plaster that first evening. They were young and sweet and nursed him with all possible care. Sometimes they would talk to him in Lithuanian, smiling when they realized he didn't understand a word. Once in a while they both came, in the company of Dr. Lustinvas, and then Bjørn heard them talking about him among themselves, the nurses' voices sounding mournful. Dr. Lustinvas would come over to his bed and stand there with a worried look in his eyes. Or he would sit down beside him, take his hand to feel his pulse or listen to his heart with the stethoscope. Every day he updated the curves on a chart that hung on the wall above his bed.

One day Dr. Lustinvas gave him an injection that made him pleasantly drowsy. Shortly afterward, Dr. Lustinvas returned, accompanied by a gentleman who spoke Norwegian, Bjørn Hansen could tell, but unfortunately he was so drowsy that he did not quite catch what the man said or wanted. Afterward, Dr. Lustinvas explained that it had been the secretary at the Norwegian embassy in Warsaw, and he pointed at the primitive bedside table which had flowers and assorted chocolates on it. At his next visit Bjørn Hansen would supposedly feel better, and the embassy secretary would bring him a bundle of Norwegian newspapers and other reading matter. Dr. Lustinvas treated Bjørn Hansen with great respect and with routine medical expertise. Bjørn also came to suspect that he had not been given ordinary hospital food but a special diet, for he could find no fault with his meals. Dr. Lustinvas alternated between giving him encouraging words and showing him sympathy. On the day when he came to report that what had occurred was irrevocable, in the sense that he must now confront the fact that he had to spend the rest of his life in a wheelchair, the doctor pressed his hands as he told him. He had sat down right beside Bjørn Hansen; indeed, he had moved his chair, which already stood near the bed, putting it exactly in such a way that, when he sat down on it, he was eye to eye with his patient. That day, too, he had a procession of nurses with him. They were lined up along the wall as he broke to Bjørn Hansen the news that there was no going back, and they stood there with grave faces, staring straight ahead and looking deeply grieved, including the two young women who had received him the first evening and who later had taken turns nursing him. They stood there in the background like a wailing Greek chorus, albeit dressed in white. Bjørn had visitors. First, the leader of the Lithuanian delegation, who lived in Vilnius, and later the secretary of the Norwegian embassy in Warsaw. During both these visits Dr. Lustinvas was present, and when the Lithuanian was there he often took the floor himself, probably telling his countryman in their common language something about the accident and its consequences for his Norwegian patient. When the embassy secretary was there, Dr. Lustinvas did not say anything, but he was there all along, in the background. This last meeting, by the way, came off very smoothly, with talk about this and that, and it was clear that the embassy secretary also was reluctant to touch directly on the reason why Bjørn Hansen found himself in a Vilnius hospital. He was Dr. Lustinvas's own patient and the doctor watched him zealously. He might suddenly pop up at Bjørn Hansen's bed, often alone. Then he would sit down and look at him, ask him how he felt and whether he found any fault with the treatment. Suddenly he would begin talking about himself. About his being a Lithuanian and a Catholic. About the Lithuanian steppes, where he had spent his childhood. About how he hated Russians and communism, yet had much to thank them for. Without them, he would not have been a doctor, but a slave of the soil. Without them, Vilnius would not have been the capital of Lithuania, but a city in Poland. "Tomorrow, perhaps, Vilnius will again be a city in Poland. It depends on the Germans. We have wandered a lot and will continue to wander. Perhaps to the banks of the Dnieper, what do I know? But if Germany wants to have Stettin and Breslau, Königsberg, Danzig and Memel back, then Poland will want to have Vilnius back and we must start wandering eastward. But I'll manage," Dr. Lustinvas added, "because God is behind it all." This is what he told his patient. This remarkable man from the rich West who was lying full length in his bed, bandaged and plastered by the book. A man to weep over, if you sat down at his bedside and reflected on what had happened, seen from the patient's point of view. But Dr. Lustinvas did not think about that. He was very vague when he touched on such things. But he was glad to sit at Bjørn Hansen's bedside. Bjørn Hansen thought that the two sweet nurses must have been initiated; they were in on the secret. But no one else needed to know anything. Only Dr. Lustinvas and two dark-haired beauties in nurse's uniforms.

Dr. Lustinvas sat by the bedside of this remarkable man, who must have transformed the doctor's life. That, perhaps, was why he came so often, in order to be in the vicinity of this man who had made an entirely new life possible for him, a future he had not even dared dream of before Bjørn Hansen showed up. The sum of $10,000 had fallen from the sky straight down into Dr. Lustinvas's lap. A wealthy man with a crazy idea in his head had turned up in his life. This bandaged and plastered man from the West was God's gift to Dr. Lustinvas, and that was also how the doctor treated Bjørn Hansen. One day Dr. Lustinvas will have to go to confession, of course, Bjørn Hansen thought, though he is not likely to do so until I've left; but will he then speak about this as a sin he has committed or as an undeserved miracle on life's journey and a blessing?

And those two little sweet nurses treated Bjørn Hansen in the same way. With great respect and much consideration. One day Dr. Lustinvas rolled a wheelchair into Bjørn Hansen's room, closely followed by both nurses. The nurses helped Bjørn Hansen into it, and after Dr. Lustinvas had instructed him in the use of it—as well as given him, in vague terms, some good advice about how a paralyzed man actually behaves, both when he is being helped into a wheelchair and when he sits in it—the two nurses rolled Bjørn Hansen out into the corridor and placed him on a covered veranda. Bjørn Hansen could then verify that spring had arrived in Lithuania. The birds were singing and the trees were sprouting fresh leaves. Soon he would leave the hospital and Vilnius. He spent yet another week there, mostly taken up with getting used to sitting in a wheelchair; he pushed himself up and down the corridors, or sat on the covered veranda with a blanket over his knees. Dr. Lustinvas would sometimes turn up as Bjørn sat there, sit beside him and explain what it meant to have been born in Lithuania. He had brought a worn photo album and showed him pictures. Of his father, the kolkhoz peasant. Of his mother, a heavyset Lithuanian country wife. Of his three brothers and his sister. He showed him a pendant of the sister, for she was dead; she died at sixteen, and so her picture was inside a pendant that Dr. Lustinvas carried on a chain around his neck. Bjørn was shown pictures of Dr. Lustinvas as a child, a young man, as a student, and as a junior doctor. Of Mrs. Lustinvas and the two children, photographed inside a cramped, overfurnished flat. Mrs. Lustinvas was also a doctor. Here in the hospital. "Too bad you haven't met her," Dr. Lustinvas said. The two children were six and eight. All the pictures looked typically stuffed, contrived. You were at the photographer's, even if the photographer was a father (of the children), husband (of Mrs. Lustinvas), or son (of his father and mother). The very interiors appeared stuffed, with all those things piled up on the rickety dining-room table around which the Lustinvas family were seated, except for Dr. Lustinvas, who took the pictures. Dr. Lustinvas dreamed of a Pax Romana: peace for the Lithuanians within the walls of the new German-Roman nation, which would check German expansion along the Baltic coast and toward the Oder-Neisse border, and in which Poles, Lithuanians and White Russians could live in eternal peace—with the Russians as the barbarians on the other side of this new Roman wall. Dr. Lustinvas's children sat at the table and stared at Bjørn. Mrs. Lustinvas stared at him. Dr. Lustinvas as a young student stared at him. He had placed his hand on the shoulder of a fellow student, and both stared at Bjørn, inscrutably. Grandmother Lustinvas stared at her son, who had returned to the countryside as a junior doctor with a camera in order to take a photograph of his mother, and from inside that picture she now stared at Bjørn Hansen, the man from the West. Dr. Lustinvas asked no questions about Bjørn Hansen's family situation. He came from the Other Side and had no history. He came to Dr. Lustinvas from outside, rich and unknown, asking a favor, and so he had changed Dr. Lustinvas's life, while he himself, for some unfathomable reason, sat in a wheelchair as a cripple. Dr. Lustinvas had no questions to ask him. Not even about the world of wealth he came from did Dr. Lustinvas ask any questions.

And so Bjørn Hansen was discharged. He was wheeled into Dr. Lustinvas's office, where he received a number of signed and stamped documents, which explained in detail his stay in Vilnius Hospital. Then he was driven to the airport. He was wheeled into the departure hall by the two dark-haired nurses. They walked side by side behind the wheelchair, each holding on to a handle while they pushed him toward the check-in window. Then one of them checked him in, while the other stood waiting behind the wheelchair. Afterward they wheeled him toward the passport check and the international departure hall, still side by side, like two sisters, behind him. At the passport check stood a Scandinavian Airlines stewardess waiting for him. The two Lithuanian nurses handed the wheelchair over to this woman, who would now bear responsibility for all further transportation. But before delivering him to the stewardess, they bent down, both of them, first one and then the other, and embraced him, while bursting into tears.

It caught them unawares, both the cool stewardess, who stepped back a little, and Bjørn Hansen, who now slumped over, anxious both about being taken through the passport check and through those long corridors to the plane. But also about what would come afterward. Meanwhile the stewardess seized the push handles of the wheelchair, wheeled him through the passport check and through a door, which then closed, and since he sat with his eyes looking straight ahead and couldn't turn round, he was no longer able to see the two nurses, who stood side by side watching him disappear through the automatic door and into his own world, which they did not even get a glimpse of before the door was closed. On the plane he was given a seat at the very back, beside a single seat reserved for the crew, where the stewardess sat down, beside him, while firmly holding the push handle of the wheelchair in one hand during the ascent. He shook his head when they brought the trolleys with food and drinks—anyway, it was "his" stewardess who was in charge of serving drinks in this section of the plane. He sat looking straight ahead, hunched up, deep in thought. He was on his way home. He had never been so afraid, and on top of that he was worried that his fear would make him tremble all over. He feared he would not be able to go through with his project. He was sitting up in the air over Europe somewhere. Inside the cramped long body of an aircraft, at the very back. He sat hunched up in a wheelchair, looking glumly straight ahead. When the plane went down for landing, the stewardess sat down in the vacant seat beside him, keeping the same firm hold on the push handle of the wheelchair. At Kastrup he was handed over to another stewardess for the last lap of the journey, between Copenhagen and Oslo. At Fornebu the personnel of an ambulance from Kongsberg Hospital took over. They were waiting as the stewardess wheeled him through the door to the open lobby, where the buzz of loud Norwegian voices hits you as you come out of the international departure hall, right after customs. He was immediately handed over to two white-clad men.

Spring had arrived in Norway, but it was cool, as he noticed during the short trip from the exit to where the ambulance was parked. It was mid-April, Tuesday of Holy Week, two days before Maundy Thursday, for Easter was late this year. He had been away for eight weeks. The ambulance drove to Kongsberg, via Drammen and Hokksund. Had he not always liked Norwegian landscapes, especially the landscape along the Drammen River, between Drammen and Hokksund, and that between Hokksund and Kongsberg, with its flat fields and steep hills? The two white-clad men sat in the front seat, telling each other what they were doing for the Easter holidays, while Bjørn Hansen sat in the back, in his wheelchair, hunched up as before. When they arrived at the Kongsberg Hospital he was carried out in the wheelchair and taken straight to Dr. Schiøtz, who was expecting him.

Dr. Schiøtz received him in a manner befitting a practiced physician: friendly but distant. There was also a nurse in the office, who assisted him. Among other things, she was helpful in transferring Bjørn Hansen from the wheelchair onto the examination table. My withered legs, Bjørn Hansen thought, remember that. But it was Dr. Schiøtz who did the examination, the nurse was never in direct contact with Bjørn Hansen's body. After the examination Bjørn Hansen was taken up to the X-ray department and Dr. Schiøtz went along. The doctor took the X-ray pictures himself, turned Bjørn Hansen over on his stomach without assistance, and afterward remained behind to wait for the developed pictures, while Bjørn Hansen was wheeled back to Dr. Schiøtz's office. Then he was alone with the nurse, but they did not talk. He lay with his eyes closed, covered by a sheet, until Dr. Schiøtz returned with the

X-rays in his hand. He looked worried. He waved to the nurse and they helped Bjørn Hansen up from the examination table and back into the wheelchair. My withered legs, Bjørn Hansen thought. Dr. Schiøtz sent the nurse out, on the pretext of fetching some documents, so they could be alone, which the nurse understood.

With an expression of concern and in a low, friendly voice brimming with sympathy, Dr. Schiøtz told him that the examination he had just undertaken fully confirmed the diagnosis made in Vilnius, a copy of which had been sent to Kongsberg Hospital. Bjørn Hansen, therefore, had to take it like a man, there was nothing else for it. Dr. Schiøtz knew it was painful to have to adjust to there being no hope, but it couldn't be helped. Dr. Schiøtz had no problem understanding that Bjørn Hansen would now slide into a state of self-pity, perhaps for months. It was entirely human, but he still hoped that Bjørn Hansen would gradually realize that life had to and could go on, with him as a participant, in a society which, after all, devoted a great many resources to enable the handicapped to live a satisfactory life.

Bjørn Hansen desperately tried to achieve eye contact with the physician. He searched for his glance, deep within. He himself sat with his eyes wide open, boring them into Dr. Schiøtz's eyes, into those eternally remote eyes, which remained remote, refusing to allow Bjørn Hansen's glance to reach him, in that he just moved his glance the moment Bjørn Hansen sought it. He heard the addicted physician tell him that society would do all it could to give Bjørn Hansen a good life. He knew that Bjørn Hansen was having a hard time now, he said, but he should know, at this moment, that the rest of them would do everything in their power to help and support him, and as he said that he turned his eyes toward the man in the wheelchair, giving him a remote but friendly glance that betrayed nothing at all of the secret they shared, which Dr. Schiøtz could have acknowledged without any cost to himself. Bjørn Hansen stared into the friendly physician's eyes, which answered his gaze with the same imperturbable friendliness. There was a gentle knock on the door and the nurse came in; she placed a pile of papers to be filled out on the doctor's desk. It was done as requested.

He was taken home to his flat. And left there. He remained alone. Bjørn Hansen sat in a wheelchair in his own flat. After a while the doorbell rang and Bjørn Hansen wheeled up to open the door. It was anything but simple. First, he had to unlock the door and leave it ajar, before turning the wheelchair around and moving back sufficiently to leave the visitor enough room to come in. It was the community nurse. A pleasant woman of about sixty who came to help him.

She asked what he would like for dinner, and when he couldn't think of anything in particular she smiled knowingly and said that, in that case, she would buy something she thought was good. She came back with a bagful of food, which he paid for. She served him salmon with cucumber salad. While he ate she walked about in the flat and smartened it up. She had bought flowers and decorations. Yellow catkins which she put on the tables and shelves. Ten yellow tulips which she put into two vases, one on the coffee table and one on the windowsill. By his plate she put a flaming yellow napkin. Now they could ring in Easter, she said. When he had finished eating, she took his plate, glass and cutlery and washed up. Then she left.

He sat in a wheelchair in a newly cleaned (Mari Ann), tidy and smartened-up flat. His son was not there, but he had left a letter. He wrote that he had found another furnished room, it was the most practical thing to do. Anyway, he had never intended to stay with him longer than necessary, only until he had got himself another place. Now he had found one in a residential area, a short distance from the town center, in the basement of a villa, where he had a bachelor flat with a private entrance. Incidentally, he would visit him one day at Easter, since he would not be going away but would stay home and read. Best regards from Peter.

At Easter a community nurse came every day and prepared food for him, did the housework and helped him with what he needed; there were two of them taking turns now and after the holiday he would become acquainted with several more. They all had a key and let themselves in. Already before Easter was over they insisted that Bjørn Hansen should try to take part in preparing his own meals—that was the best way, they said, one had to try to do as much as possible oneself—"It's for your own good. Being self-reliant gives you a positive attitude toward life," they said.

One day the doorbell rang. Twice. But Bjørn Hansen didn't open. For some reason or other he got the idea that it might be Turid Lammers and he didn't want to see her. He hadn't seen her in the five years since he moved out of the Lammers villa, apart from a few times at a considerable distance, and then he had turned around or made a detour. Nor had she looked him up, but it occurred to him nevertheless that it could be Turid Lammers when the doorbell rang. She was bound to be driven by a deep need to see him, with her own eyes, sitting in a wheelchair. And then they could have resigned themselves, she to her pity, he to his purification. He would do everything in his power not to be seen, and to avoid talking to Turid Lammers in his present physical condition. But it did not need to have been Turid Lammers who rang the bell. It could, for example, have been Herman Busk. But he wouldn't open for him either. Not now. Not yet.

However, it had not been Herman Busk. He rang up right after Easter and had been away at the time. He wanted to come over and see Bjørn Hansen, but Bjørn Hansen told him that, honestly, he wasn't up to it yet, he must become stronger first, and Herman Busk understood. But a week later he rang again, and then about once a week for some time. Bjørn Hansen declined to meet him, but for entirely different reasons from the one he had for avoiding Turid Lammers.

Some time after Easter he wheeled himself through the streets to the Town Hall, where the Treasury was located. He had no problems traveling by wheelchair through the streets of Kongsberg, neither physically nor psychologically. He greeted some remote acquaintances and they returned his greeting as naturally as they could. At the Town Hall he managed to get in on the ground floor, but not higher up, to the second floor, where the Treasury was. Instead of making the effort of carrying the wheelchair with him in it up to the second floor, his subordinates came down to the ground floor, where he had maneuvered himself into the space behind the information counter. There he was served coffee, also rolls and Danish pastry, which the junior clerk had been sent out in a hurry to buy. They said he looked very well.

As he was about to say goodbye and wheel himself out onto the street again, the alderman came, so he had a conversation with him, while the Treasury employees went back to their work. After a bit of waffling, during which the alderman inquired whether his sense of humor was still intact (I'll be damned if I ever distinguished myself by a great sense of humor here in the Town Hall, Bjørn Hansen thought gruffly), he came to the matter at hand. About what would happen when the period of his sick leave had expired. The alderman assumed that Bjørn Hansen would then apply for a disability pension, so that they could start the process of appointing a new treasurer without delay. In the alderman's opinion, Jorunn Meck stood out as a very interesting candidate, what did Bjørn Hansen think of that? Bjørn Hansen was taken aback. He had no intention of resigning as treasurer. He had taken it for granted that he would continue as before—after all, nothing stood in his way except for the practical problem of getting from the ground floor to the first. But to the alderman it seemed all but indisputable that Bjørn Hansen would resign as treasurer now that he was disabled. He said, however, that there was no need for him to be completely cut off from the Town Hall milieu. "We would like to take advantage of your expertise as a consultant," he said. Bjørn said nothing to that. If he had been genuinely disabled, he would have protested most sharply, but not now, he simply didn't have the strength. His head swimming, he wheeled himself out of the Town Hall and through the streets to his flat on the other side of New Bridge.

Home. In his own flat. In a wheelchair. The former treasurer of Kongsberg. Fifty-one years of age. The days went by. Time passed. The community nursing office was very satisfied with him. They thought he showed a positive attitude. He demonstrated a strong desire to master the small everyday problems by himself, and in an astonishingly short time he was able to do the shopping, prepare his meals, do the dishes and the laundry himself (except for awkward items like bed linen and the like). All that remained for the home help to do once a week was the cleaning (Mari Ann had quit and would sit her A levels in the spring) and the heavy laundry. However, a community nurse visited him once every twenty-four hours. To check on him, in case he should need help with something, which might well be the case. For example, to fetch a book from a top shelf. Or something could have happened to him which left him helpless. The days went by. Time passes. The high point of the day was the expedition to the supermarket to do the shopping. First, the laborious operation of getting through the door of his own flat. Then into and out of the lift. Next, to get through the front door and fairly sail along the street to the supermarket, where it was cool and the floor was level and pleasant to roll along on. In the mornings there were few customers; he was almost alone among the mountains of merchandise. He wheeled his way down the aisles as though he were in the middle of a street, with enormous accumulations of, say, toothpaste, detergents, oranges, salami, cheese, milk, green apples, red apples and hamburgers on both sides. He took his time in there, sometimes more than an hour, rolling back and forth in the streets of the supermarket and picking up what he needed. He came to know the staff very well, both the women at the checkout and those who ran about supplying the shelves with constantly fresh tomatoes, mince, cream, fabric conditioner. He had the impression that they liked him. He was a kind of dignified invalid. Not obtrusively noisy or cheerful. Not steeped in suffering. But friendly and resigned in all his dealings.

Sometimes he would also wheel himself down to Lågen to look at the river. Or he rolled about the streets. Then he would often strike up a conversation with old acquaintances, who all seemed relieved that he had confronted his fate with such composure. Did that make him feel ashamed? No, he considered their reactions with an inexpressible remoteness. About the same as when his son visited him, just after Easter. If the doorbell rang now, he opened the door. The worry that Turid Lammers might be standing outside he now regarded as fanciful. And Herman Busk would not come. He spoke to Bjørn Hansen by telephone. Then Bjørn could interrupt the conversation if he felt something emerge from deep down that made it impossible for him to continue. Outside the door a seller of raffle tickets or a child might be standing. Or sometimes the community nurse (one of three women), or the home help, a black man about thirty who came once a week. Did he fear being found out? Not at all. For that, his case was too unbelievable. He did not have to sit on tenterhooks when visited by the community nurse, wondering whether he behaved correctly at every moment. Even if he should get excited or be careless, make movements that a trained nurse knew were incompatible with the movements a man who was paralyzed from his hips down could possibly make, she would never have registered it. For the possibility that he might do it did not exist for her, so that, even if she had seen something, she would still not have seen anything. Indeed, even if she had seen him get halfway to his feet in the wheelchair to reach a volume in the bookcase, she would not have believed her own eyes. Of that he was absolutely certain.

Dr. Schiøtz was behind all the arrangements that made it

possible for Bjørn Hansen to live without the least fear of being found out. It was the doctor who had explained to him that he had nothing to fear, not even from the first examination at the hospital, when Dr. Schiøtz coldly and calmly allowed a nurse to assist him. And, indeed, the nurse had suspected nothing, even though she had helped lift the town treasurer out of his wheelchair and onto the examination table. Although Bjørn Hansen had concentrated intensely on simulating a paralyzed person, he was still an amateur and could easily have been found out by a nurse's sharp eye, if such vigilance had been within the bounds of possibility in such a situation; the secret happened to be, of course, that it was not.

It was Dr. Schiøtz who had arranged everything; Bjørn Hansen was the actor who performed his simulations, but according to Dr. Schiøtz's instructions and convincing interpretations. However, the most important of the physician's arrangements were those that he undertook in order to prevent Bjørn Hansen from coming into contact with anyone who might have been able to unmask him. Other doctors, in the absence of Dr. Schiøtz, ergotherapists and physiotherapists. In other words, to prevent Bjørn Hansen from having to stay in a convalescence home and being subjected to rehabilitation and expert training programs. Sunnaas Hospital was a threat, which only Dr. Schiøtz's authority prevented Bjørn Hansen from becoming acquainted with. Dr. Schiøtz pointed out that it was unnecessary to send the patient there, a training program at home was an equally effective solution and much less expensive—an argument that proved irresistible. In order to hinder a Kongsberg physiotherapist from treating Bjørn Hansen, however, Dr. Schiøtz had to do a bit of juggling, he had told him, but it would work out all right and not be discovered, unless this whole case were to unravel for other reasons.

Bjørn Hansen found himself in a wheelchair. In his own flat. Wheeled himself about in the flat, letting time pass. Enjoyed looking forward to his strenuous expeditions to the cool spaces and streets of the supermarket. He could not complain. In fact, that would be quite unthinkable. This had been his plan, which he had put into effect. However, fundamentally, he was the creation of Dr. Schiøtz.

With more than a touch of displeasure, he began to look upon himself as an artwork signed *Dr. Schiøtz*. Bjørn Hansen now realized that Dr. Schiøtz had knowingly chained him to a wheelchair, for life. He could have prevented it (when Bjørn Hansen was sent from Vilnius to his Kongsberg Hospital office in a wheelchair on the Tuesday of Holy Week, he could, once the two of them were alone, have said, "We'll stop now," and then Bjørn Hansen could have gone no further), but he did not dare to. On the contrary, he pushed on, inexorably. In an unendurable atmosphere (a "dangerous game") he had staged that last journey over to the Other Side, from which there was no return without catastrophic consequences for both of them (and for Dr. Lustinvas). Up to this point they would both have gone free (although not Dr. Lustinvas): Dr. Schiøtz because he would have exposed Bjørn Hansen's deception and left no clues that pointed back to him (in case Bjørn Hansen should try to implicate him, as a hypothetical possibility); and Bjørn Hansen because he had obviously gone mad and consequently would have been reported ill and consigned to psychiatric treatment before he could resume his position as treasurer of

Kongsberg. But instead, Dr. Schiøtz had carried out the plan mercilessly, without even asking Bjørn Hansen if he really wanted to go on, in those few seconds before it became serious and he was committed to it for life. It was as if Dr. Schiøtz feared that Bjørn Hansen, who after all sat in a wheelchair and knew he would remain there, even though he did not need to, but had to if he took this last little step without protesting about it, might nonetheless give the alarm at the last moment, before this preposterous and dangerous game had turned serious. What were Dr. Schiøtz's motives? What forces could be driving him?

Why had Dr. Schiøtz forced this through? What possible joy could it give him to chain a healthy person to a wheelchair in this way? It was certainly not in order to see him sitting there, for at the beginning of September Bjørn Hansen could report that he had not seen Dr. Schiøtz since the "examination" at Kongsberg Hospital five months ago. At first he had thought it was because Dr. Schiøtz refused to take the risk of calling on him because someone, say, the community nurse, might then "surprise" them together. But why would that have mattered? A doctor calling on one of his patients, what suspicion could be aroused by that? None at all, at least not if they were "surprised" only once, which would not be very probable, even if Dr. Schiøtz had visited Bjørn Hansen both often and regularly. But Dr. Schiøtz had called him. He had spoken to the doctor on the telephone. Three times in the last two months. He had then been the caring doctor who rang up to encourage him. In a gentle voice he had asked how he was doing, and when Bjørn Hansen had replied that "life must go on," he had praised him. He had given him sound advice about building up the strength in his arms, because now the arms alone must, after all, replace much of what arms and legs jointly had done so simply and efficiently before. Finally he had asked about some practical matters, such as the fact that Bjørn Hansen, on the alderman's recommendation, had applied for a disability pension, besides asking about whether Bjørn Hansen had received the insurance money he was entitled to. It was no great sum, only 160,000 kroner, ordinary travel insurance. But by inquiring about it—as he did every time he called—Dr. Schiøtz was hinting at what bound their fates together, because it had been part of their agreement that Dr. Schiøtz would receive half of the insurance money. In fact, at some point during the planning stage they had discussed whether Bjørn Hansen should take out a larger insurance but had decided against it, because it was too risky to take out an insurance of that size shortly before the accident it was to cover occurred. But by referring to this modest travel insurance every time he called, Dr. Schiøtz had given Bjørn Hansen a secret sign that he had not "forgotten" him or repressed their common project, which had now been realized, but that he still felt bound by it, which Bjørn Hansen heard with a sense of relief.

At the beginning of September the insurance company informed him that the money had been released and deposited in his bank account. He had the community nurse take out 20,000 kroner. A few days later he contacted Peter and had him take out 25,000 kroner, of which he gave his son 5,000 kroner, which made him very happy. He met his son in front of Kongsberg Engineering College, on the open plaza there, which was flooded by a bright autumn light; sitting in his wheelchair, a plaid over his knees, he handed his son 5,000 kroner before rolling home again. He rang up Dr. Schiøtz at the hospital. During their conversation he mentioned that the insurance money had arrived. Then he put 40,000 kroner in an envelope and waited. Dr. Schiøtz came the same evening.

Bjørn Hansen received the doctor sitting in his wheelchair; he opened the door to him in his laborious way and rolled ahead of him into the living room. Dr. Schiøtz met his own creation, which at the same time was Bjørn Hansen's own project. This meeting ended in dismay for Bjørn Hansen, for when Dr. Schiøtz had left, Bjørn Hansen remained behind, totally isolated and with a picture of himself that really gave him a fright. At first he had been disappointed because his attempt at achieving contact with the doctor was rejected. Every invitation to a mutual understanding was refused. Dr. Schiøtz was on a mild high and all he was interested in was the money. What Bjørn Hansen had understood as a formal confirmation of their pact—in the sense that Bjørn Hansen, by giving Dr. Schiøtz the envelope, had fulfilled his obligations and Dr. Schiøtz, by receiving it, confirmed that he, for his part, had taken on these obligations, so that the handing over of the money was to be seen as a symbolic act that bound them ever closer to each other—was lost on Dr. Schiøtz; for him *the money* was the main thing, and the only reason why he happened to be there. This was obvious from his behavior. Looking restlessly about him, his face lit up when he caught sight of the envelope, which Bjørn Hansen had laid on top of the sideboard, the sole item there. "Is that . . . ?" asked the doctor, and when Bjørn Hansen nodded he snatched the envelope. He put it in his inside pocket and looked at his watch. "Very sorry," he said, "but I have to go now. I have an important appointment."

Bjørn Hansen looked at him—that was the moment when he felt dismayed.

For this didn't make sense. It was just a game. It wasn't about the money. From the very start there had always been something evasive about Dr. Schiøtz in regard to his cut of the money. As a condition of joining in, he had then said that he must have half of the insurance. But soon afterward he had rejected the idea of taking out a more lucrative insurance, because it was too risky. But was it? Bjørn Hansen didn't think so; no great risk anyway. But regardless, Dr. Schiøtz was not willing to take *any* risk so that he might be able to stuff, let's say, a million kroner straight into his pocket. But for a paltry 80,000 he sets to work. And is extremely eager to get his hands on the money. Rings up three times to ask if it has arrived. And when it does arrive he comes at once. It didn't add up, not at all. Was he trying to make Bjørn Hansen think he had done it for the money? For 80,000 kroner? What was 80,000 kroner to Dr. Schiøtz? Nothing. True, he was a drug addict, but he got his drugs from the hospital, free of charge. He had plenty of money and, besides, he had in no way, in all the years Bjørn Hansen had known him, given the impression of being greedy or tightfisted. So why was he now trying to make Bjørn Hansen believe that this was exactly what he was—that he would do practically anything for 80,000 kroner?

Dr. Schiøtz was looking for a motive he could live with, that was the only explanation Bjørn Hansen could see. To live with, vis-à-vis himself and vis-à-vis Bjørn Hansen. But also, in the last resort, the crux of the matter, Bjørn Hansen presumed: to live with if he fell and was ruined, if, that is, the whole affair should somehow or other come to light. And there was only one way it could come to light now: if either Bjørn Hansen or Dr. Schiøtz "cracked." If the doctor did, he would need a motive in order to explain his actions. Then he could say he had done it for the money, and Bjørn Hansen could confirm that, because he had noted Dr. Schiøtz's behavior: the fact that he came as soon as Bjørn Hansen had obtained the money and that the money was the only thing he was thinking about. The doctor's motive was greed, financial gain. And this, of course, society would swallow, because it was so despicable that nobody would think of admitting it unless forced to do so. Yet Dr. Schiøtz found it absolutely necessary to cling to this despicable and untrue motive. If he were exposed he was finished, ruined, he knew that full well. Nevertheless he found it necessary, when he imagined himself finished, ruined, unmasked, to be able to say that he had done it for money. And for that he now needed Bjørn Hansen. To confirm his alleged motive after an imagined exposure, something so important to him that he was prepared to increase the risk of being exposed. For the chance that Bjørn Hansen might "crack" was, of course, increased considerably now that, from Dr. Schiøtz's viewpoint, it must have dawned on him that Dr. Schiøtz was not a fellow conspirator, someone he was morally obliged to protect, with the consequence that he must never "crack," because then his coconspirator would be ruined, but someone who went along purely for the money, even if he might have had a certain intellectual curiosity about the project, Bjørn Hansen supposed Dr. Schiøtz thought that Bjørn Hansen was now thinking. But why was this so important to him? It could only mean that Dr. Schiøtz did not want to have his real motives exposed to public scrutiny. He had done it for money. Not because he . . . Oh, what *were* Dr. Schiøtz's motives!

Bjørn Hansen had no way of knowing. But he knew they were of such a nature that Dr. Schiøtz could not acknowledge them even to himself. He could acknowledge, if necessary, that he had condemned Bjørn Hansen to a wheelchair because he was willing to do so, for money, but not for anything else. That was when the true horror of this act dawned on Bjørn Hansen. Who was Bjørn Hansen? Who sat (voluntarily) in a wheelchair? What was so terrible about Dr. Schiøtz, his fellow conspirator, preferring to be judged as a despicable and greedy human being rather than have the spotlight thrown upon what was really at stake?

"It's only half the amount," Bjørn Hansen said, limply. "It's 40,000, not 80,000. I won't risk withdrawing more. Not for the time being. You'll get the rest in six months." The doctor looked at him and nodded. "That's all right," he said. He stood there shifting from one foot to another, eager to get going. Bjørn Hansen threw up his hands. "Let's say six months from today. Same place, same time." Dr. Schiøtz nodded. He said a brief goodbye, without any pretence at being the thoughtful doctor visiting his patient. After Dr. Schiøtz had left, Bjørn Hansen remained alone. He was afraid of his own fate. He was completely alone, but someone else's creation. He was someone else's creation, but that someone else did not dare to be confronted by his handiwork—not in the eyes of others, nor in his own. What had he done? What was so terrible about this that even Dr. Schiøtz had to prepare an escape route from the accusation that he was a party to Bjørn Hansen's project? What was so frightening about Bjørn Hansen sitting voluntarily in a wheelchair, and about Dr. Schiøtz having been instrumental in putting him there? To the doctor himself? Was it his motivation, or was it the act itself? Was it his reason for doing it, or was it the horror of Bjørn Hansen sitting in a wheelchair of his own free will? The reason for his involvement must, after all, have been similar to Bjørn Hansen's own, although there is a difference between being a party to someone else placing himself in such a situation and actually being that someone else, Bjørn Hansen thought. He no longer gave much consideration to his own motives. He could no longer remember why he had been so obsessed with this idea. He knew he *had* been obsessed, but could no longer explain why. He sat there trying to think back, to find the thread that made him actually go through with it. It certainly wasn't the life of a wheelchair user that fascinated him. Nor was it the thought of sitting in a wheelchair pretending to be paralyzed when he wasn't and thereby fooling everyone. It was not the irresistible fascination of making a fool of society—his friends, acquaintances, even his own son—that had driven him to this. What was it, then? He did not know. But he had done it. And when he thought about having done it and remembered the insane attraction he had felt when the idea struck him, he could accept that, deep inside, he felt a profound satisfaction at having carried out this act, which was now a fait accompli, and this profound satisfaction corresponded perfectly to the fascination he had felt at the thought that it was possible to carry out such an act, like an echo, an inward confirmation, a continuity, like a river that had finally found its course and now flowed calmly, unseen, through his innermost self. He had no problem dismissing any conception or idea he might have, and would continue to have, which might present a rational or praiseworthy explanation for it, because there was no such explanation. Every time he had tried, he would dismiss it mercilessly after a while. To call this act an "exploit" or a "revolt," or a "challenge," appeared to him to be pompous and slightly ridiculous. And he was incapable of seeing anything wonderful in being able to fool people into believing that he was paralyzed and had to sit in a wheelchair when in reality there was nothing wrong with him (apart from his stomach, which still throbbed, and his teeth, which also still throbbed); it was really just stupid, embarrassing even, especially considering that he was drawing on society's resources and subjecting people in the public health service, who were on the whole warmhearted, often idealistic human beings, to a practical joke that in the cold light of day gave him a shameful, almost sickening taste in his mouth. Nevertheless, there was something about his having carried out this act that filled him with a moist, dark peace. That he neither could nor would deny, and it did not cease or come to an end even if Dr. Schiøtz's horror at this very same act also horrified him, in addition to his having to accept that now it was all up to him, as he sat there in his mute loneliness, to endure the sight of this act, which had given him insight, in a wholly fundamental way, into what is hidden behind the concept "to be led straight into perdition," with open eyes.

Yes, the meeting with Dr. Schiøtz had given him a jolt. He was truly alone with it now. In his flat. Day and night. But then the telephone rang. It was Herman Busk. Bjørn Hansen was glad. Perhaps Herman Busk picked this up, for he at once invited Bjørn over for Sunday dinner, which he accepted with thanks. He had not seen Herman Busk since the "accident," having felt reluctant to do so, although Herman Busk had often hinted that they ought to be able to see each other again, rather than just talk on the telephone. But now he had said yes.

Herman Busk picked him up on Sunday. He came up to the flat, which they left together, took the lift to the ground floor and entered the street. Herman Busk pushed him along the streets and roads to his villa in one of Kongsberg's old residential areas. It was a fine sunny autumn day; the leaves on the trees had acquired a smoldering glow. There was a slightly nippy air, which had an enlivening effect on Bjørn Hansen in his wheelchair as he was rolled along by his friend Herman Busk. Herman Busk also seemed in high spirits, glad anyway. He spoke in a light and lively manner as he pushed the wheelchair along. When they arrived at the dentist's home, Herman Busk rolled him carefully up the gravel-covered driveway. He maneuvered him up the stairs, carefully and by fits and starts, and entered the hallway. Berit came to welcome him. Wearing an apron, she emerged through the door to the kitchen, from whence came a delicious fragrance of roast lamb. Herman Busk wheeled Bjørn Hansen into the drawing room, where the two gentlemen partook of some refreshment before dinner. Meanwhile Bjørn could hear and see Berit bustling about, sometimes in the kitchen, sometimes in the dining room, where she was putting the finishing touches to the table. Finally she came out and announced that dinner was served. Herman Busk got up and pushed Bjørn Hansen into the dining room. There the table was set, the same way he had seen it a hundred times before, except that where his chair had been there was now an empty hole, into which Herman Busk wheeled him. White tablecloth. An attractive china dinner set, crystal glasses, silver cutlery, and a white damask napkin nicely folded at each place setting. Herman Busk sat down in his usual seat. Berit brought in the dishes. Roast lamb, white beans and roast potatoes. Juice from the lamb for sauce. Simple and flavorsome. Berit insisted, now as before, on roasting the lamb a little more than was customary nowadays, so it was well done, and not pink inside, and although Bjørn Hansen usually preferred it pink, there was nevertheless nothing that could compare to Berit's roast lamb, that he knew from experience, and now he was really looking forward to the meal. Herman Busk poured red wine and the dishes were passed around. Sunday dinner at Kongsberg, in the home of Busk, the dentist.

Conversation came easy and was carefree, as it should be. Berit and Herman Busk were both radiant at having their old guest and friend back at the dinner table again. But in the middle of the meal Bjørn Hansen felt that he had to go to the lavatory. He grew annoyed with himself—he could have remembered to go at home before Herman Busk came to pick him up, but he had no doubt been too excited. Now he tried to hold himself back, but after a while he had to admit that it wouldn't work. He was very sorry. "It causes so much commotion, and it's no fun for you either," he said when Herman Busk got up and wheeled him out to the lavatory. There they confronted a fresh ordeal. The lavatory was too small to accommodate the wheelchair. As opposed to Bjørn Hansen's flat, Herman Busk's house was not adapted to wheelchair users (Bjørn Hansen lived in a modern block of flats from the mid-1980s where disabled access was part of the regulations. If I hadn't lived in that flat I would probably never have come up with the idea that has led me to where I am now, Bjørn Hansen had often thought, half jokingly). Herman Busk was desperate. He looked at Bjørn Hansen in bewilderment. "I'll manage," Bjørn Hansen said, "but I would like to be alone."

Herman Busk opened the door to the lavatory, placed the wheelchair with Bjørn Hansen in it by the wall and quickly left. He returned to the dining room, while Bjørn Hansen quietly got out of the wheelchair. He walked, on tiptoe, into the lavatory. It was the first time he had done this, having all along been particular about following the rules of the game, even when he was all alone in his flat and had been faced by some pretty demanding tasks, from the point of view of a wheelchair user. But now he had got up and was pissing, standing bolt upright as if it were the most natural thing in the world.

The Busks were waiting in the dining room. Out here Bjørn Hansen stood bolt upright pissing. What if they knew! Suddenly Bjørn Hansen felt an intense desire that Herman Busk should inadvertently come into the hall and see him standing there pissing. It wouldn't have been so improbable. Herman Busk must certainly have wondered whether Bjørn Hansen had managed to get to the lavatory on his own or whether he should perhaps help, in spite of everything. But it was impossible. Herman Busk would never have been so tactless. Bjørn Hansen had asked to be left alone and Herman Busk understood why. He did not want to be seen in a humiliating position, like, for example, crawling along the floor toward the lavatory and hoisting himself onto the toilet seat, then making his way back again in the same humiliating (because someone was watching) way. He could trust Herman Busk. He knew that he and Berit sat in the dining room, at the dinner table, paying close attention, listening, ready to come running if they heard a crash (as he fell) and understood that he needed help. But otherwise not. He was completely confident of not being found out as he stood there, bolt upright, as if it were the most natural thing in the world.

Nevertheless, he was not able to relinquish his intense desire to be seen. By his friend Herman Busk, who would suddenly turn up in the hall and see him stand there, exactly as he had been before the "accident" had struck him down so senselessly. He was certain that Herman Busk would understand. Hssh, Bjørn would have whispered as he pressed his forefinger to his lips in front of a gaping Herman Busk, who could scarcely believe his eyes. But when Bjørn Hansen made the sign for hssh, Herman Busk would have pulled himself together, nodded, and made a sign in return, with his hands, to indicate that he was happily surprised. He would become an initiate—and what more could Bjørn Hansen wish for himself than to initiate his friend Herman Busk into this incomprehensible thing that he had imposed on himself? Perhaps they could initiate Berit, too, although this was something Bjørn Hansen was less certain of. But Herman Busk would understand him. Not *why* he had done it, but *that* he had done it, and because he had done it he would accept it and let himself be initiated into it. Bjørn Hansen was certain that Herman Busk would understand it and accept it. If he stood here long enough, Herman Busk would sooner or later come out, for if Bjørn did not return, he and Mrs. Busk would exchange uneasy glances, and Herman would have to overcome his reluctance to go out there and possibly see his friend in a situation he did not want to be seen in and which, accordingly, Herman Busk did not want to see his friend in. But something must have happened now, since it was so quiet out there and Bjørn had not returned. If I stand here long enough, Bjørn Hansen thought, my friend will sooner or later come out and see me, and I will have an ally in my life. But he refrained from doing that. He finished his piss, shook his prick, walked (on tiptoe) into the hall and quietly got back into his wheelchair. It would not have been right to do it. What he did was not right either, but this was what his life had become. He could not change that, not for a beautiful (and maybe dubious) dream that his friend might become an ally. His fate was to live without anyone being initiated into the hair-raising fact that he sat in a wheelchair as if paralyzed without being so. He wheeled the chair down the narrow hallway and into the dining room, where Herman Busk had opened the door wide in anticipation of his coming back. Their faces lit up when they saw their unfortunate friend, who had at long last chosen to return as a guest in their home.

New Directions Paperbooks—a partial listing

Kaouther Adimi, Our Riches
Adonis, Songs of Mihyar the Damascene
César Aira, Artforum
An Episode in the Life of a Landscape Painter
Ghosts
Will Alexander, The Sri Lankan Loxodrome
Osama Alomar, The Teeth of the Comb
Guillaume Apollinaire, Selected Writings
Paul Auster, The Red Notebook
White Spaces
Ingeborg Bachmann, Malina
Honoré de Balzac, Colonel Chabert
Djuna Barnes, Nightwood
Charles Baudelaire, The Flowers of Evil*
Bei Dao, City Gate, Open Up
Mei-Mei Berssenbrugge, Empathy
Max Blecher, Adventures in Immediate Irreality
Roberto Bolaño, By Night in Chile
Distant Star
Jorge Luis Borges, Labyrinths
Seven Nights
Coral Bracho, Firefly Under the Tongue*
Kamau Brathwaite, Ancestors
Basil Bunting, Complete Poems
Anne Carson, Glass, Irony & God
Norma Jeane Baker of Troy
Horacio Castellanos Moya, Senselessness
Camilo José Cela, Mazurka for Two Dead Men
Louis-Ferdinand Céline
Death on the Installment Plan
Journey to the End of the Night
Rafael Chirbes, On the Edge
Inger Christensen, alphabet
Julio Cortázar, All Fires the Fire
Cronopios & Famas
Jonathan Creasy, ed: Black Mountain Poems
Robert Creeley, If I Were Writing This
Guy Davenport, 7 Greeks
Osamu Dazai, No Longer Human
H. D., Selected Poems
Helen DeWitt, The Last Samurai
Some Trick
Marcia Douglas
The Marvellous Equations of the Dread
Daša Drndić, EEG
Robert Duncan, Selected Poems
Eça de Queirós, The Maias
William Empson, 7 Types of Ambiguity
Mathias Énard, Compass
Tell Them of Battles, Kings & Elephants
Shusaku Endo, Deep River
Jenny Erpenbeck, The End of Days
Go, Went, Gone
Lawrence Ferlinghetti
A Coney Island of the Mind
F. Scott Fitzgerald, The Crack-Up
On Booze
Jean Frémon, Now, Now, Louison
Rivka Galchen, Little Labors
Forrest Gander, Be With
Romain Gary, The Kites
Natalia Ginzburg, The Dry Heart
Happiness, as Such
Henry Green, Concluding
Felisberto Hernández, Piano Stories
Hermann Hesse, Siddhartha
Takashi Hiraide, The Guest Cat
Yoel Hoffmann, Moods
Susan Howe, My Emily Dickinson
Debths
Bohumil Hrabal, I Served the King of England
Qurratulain Hyder, River of Fire
Sonallah Ibrahim, That Smell
Rachel Ingalls, Binstead's Safari
Mrs. Caliban
Christopher Isherwood, The Berlin Stories
Fleur Jaeggy, Sweet Days of Discipline
Alfred Jarry, Ubu Roi
B. S. Johnson, House Mother Normal
James Joyce, Stephen Hero
Franz Kafka, Amerika: The Man Who Disappeared
Investigations of a Dog
Yasunari Kawabata, Dandelions
John Keene, Counternarratives
Heinrich von Kleist, Michael Kohlhaas
Alexander Kluge, Temple of the Scapegoat
Taeko Kono, Toddler-Hunting
Laszlo Krasznahorkai, Satantango
Seiobo There Below
Ryszard Krynicki, Magnetic Point
Eka Kurniawan, Beauty Is a Wound
Mme. de Lafayette, The Princess of Clèves
Lautréamont, Maldoror
Siegfried Lenz, The German Lesson
Denise Levertov, Selected Poems

Li Po, Selected Poems
Clarice Lispector, The Hour of the Star
The Passion According to G. H.
Federico García Lorca, Selected Poems*
Three Tragedies
Nathaniel Mackey, Splay Anthem
Xavier de Maistre, Voyage Around My Room
Stéphane Mallarmé, Selected Poetry and Prose*
Javier Marías, Your Face Tomorrow (3 volumes)
Bernadette Mayer, The Bernadette Mayer Reader
Midwinter Day
Carson McCullers, The Member of the Wedding
Thomas Merton, New Seeds of Contemplation
The Way of Chuang Tzu
Henri Michaux, A Barbarian in Asia
Dunya Mikhail, The Beekeeper
Henry Miller, The Colossus of Maroussi
Big Sur & the Oranges of Hieronymus Bosch
Yukio Mishima, Confessions of a Mask
Death in Midsummer
Star
Eugenio Montale, Selected Poems*
Vladimir Nabokov, Laughter in the Dark
Nikolai Gogol
The Real Life of Sebastian Knight
Pablo Neruda, The Captain's Verses*
Love Poems*
Charles Olson, Selected Writings
Mary Oppen, Meaning a Life
George Oppen, New Collected Poems
Wilfred Owen, Collected Poems
Hiroko Oyamada, The Factory
Michael Palmer, The Laughter of the Sphinx
Nicanor Parra, Antipoems*
Boris Pasternak, Safe Conduct
Kenneth Patchen
Memoirs of a Shy Pornographer
Octavio Paz, Poems of Octavio Paz
Victor Pelevin, Omon Ra
Alejandra Pizarnik
Extracting the Stone of Madness
Ezra Pound, The Cantos
New Selected Poems and Translations
Raymond Queneau, Exercises in Style
Qian Zhongshu, Fortress Besieged
Raja Rao, Kanthapura
Herbert Read, The Green Child
Kenneth Rexroth, Selected Poems
Keith Ridgway, Hawthorn & Child
Rainer Maria Rilke
Poems from the Book of Hours
Arthur Rimbaud, Illuminations*
A Season in Hell and The Drunken Boat*
Evelio Rosero, The Armies
Fran Ross, Oreo
Joseph Roth, The Emperor's Tomb
The Hotel Years
Raymond Roussel, Locus Solus
Ihara Saikaku, The Life of an Amorous Woman
Nathalie Sarraute, Tropisms
Jean-Paul Sartre, Nausea
Delmore Schwartz
In Dreams Begin Responsibilities
Hasan Shah, The Dancing Girl
W.G. Sebald, The Emigrants
The Rings of Saturn
Anne Serre, The Governesses
Stevie Smith, Best Poems
Gary Snyder, Turtle Island
Dag Solstad, Professor Andersen's Night
Muriel Spark, The Driver's Seat
Loitering with Intent
Antonio Tabucchi, Pereira Maintains
Junichiro Tanizaki, The Maids
Yoko Tawada, The Emissary
Memoirs of a Polar Bear
Dylan Thomas, A Child's Christmas in Wales
Collected Poems
Uwe Timm, The Invention of Curried Sausage
Tomas Tranströmer, The Great Enigma
Leonid Tsypkin, Summer in Baden-Baden
Tu Fu, Selected Poems
Paul Valéry, Selected Writings
Enrique Vila-Matas, Bartleby & Co.
Elio Vittorini, Conversations in Sicily
Rosmarie Waldrop, Gap Gardening
Robert Walser, The Assistant
The Tanners
The Walk
Eliot Weinberger, An Elemental Thing
The Ghosts of Birds
Nathanael West, The Day of the Locust
Miss Lonelyhearts
Tennessee Williams, The Glass Menagerie
A Streetcar Named Desire
William Carlos Williams, Selected Poems
Spring and All
Louis Zukofsky, "A"

*BILINGUAL EDITION